BRODY BOONDOGGLE

The LAST AKAWAY

A Spirit Animal Adventure

GARY KARTON

Illustrated by Samuel Valentino

BRATTLE
PUBLISHING GROUP

Library of Congress Cataloging-in-Publication Data is Available

ISBN: 13: 978-0-9854295-0-8
ISBN: 10: 098542950X

Printed in the United States of America
First edition, March 2013

Book Design by Bumblecat Design and Illustration
Illustrations by Samuel Valentino

Dedication

To Jake and Brody. And to Halea, too.

Acknowledgments

I've often been criticized for taking the opinions of kids too seriously. Well, I want to start by thanking all the kids who believed in this book when the adults didn't.

That starts with Jake, Brody, and Alec. I knew I was on to something after Jake, who is living proof that special powers really do exist, finished an early draft and said, "I hoped I would like it, but I didn't expect to like it this much." Brody, a beautiful reader (just one of his many gifts), graciously reviewed every draft at least once. And believe me, there were plenty of drafts during the four years it took to get this book published. And Alec, who was one of the two people outside of my family who was consistently passionate about this project. He was always there to brainstorm or give an honest opinion such as, "You're going to absolutely ruin this book, but hey, it's your book." Dave was the other. Everyone should be lucky enough to have a friend like Dave.

Thanks to all the other kids who read the book and helped make it better. Jared, whose opinion and backflip I totally respect. Canon, who not only read the book but also made an awesome video to help promote it. Maddie, who is one of my favorite kids who I barely get to see, and her sister, Grace, who is everything I think is great about kids. I gave a draft to Frances at 10 p.m. one night. I saw her the next morning on a snow day and she said, "Great book." She stayed up late to read it. Thanks to CeCe, who will be psyched to learn the book is finally getting published—although now we won't have anything to talk about. Thanks to Hannah and Jonathon for saying it was one of their favorites—they're lucky enough to have a dad who introduces them to all kinds of books. And all the other kids, including Moussa, Bou, Alexandre, Chris, Lucy, Willie, and Christina, who read one draft or another just to make sure I was still on the right track.

I'm not sure if Zach ever read the entire book, but he's so cool I have to include him. The same goes for Brian, Jaylan, Morgan, Tyler, Colby, Connor, Sophie (both of them), Brady, Kai, and Lainey.

Of course, there are some adults who helped as well. Thanks, Mark and Jacki, for sharing all your creativity. Karen Rosenblum, an amazing person and one of my favorite adults who I barely get to see. Gordon and Gretchen, who are always helping someone. Susan DeLaurentis is about as cool as it gets. She hooked me up with Eric Delabarre, who could not have been more generous with his time and expertise. Thank you, Charlie, for proofreading the manuscript twice even though you don't believe in the magic of magic. Rachel has a million things going on but still took the time to give me notes. I can't wait until you produce the movie.

Thanks to my agent, Michele Mortimer, at Darhansoff & Verrill, for her time and advice even when she didn't have to give it, and also Lisa Leshne for being the first person in the industry to love the story. A special thanks to Susan, Skeeta, Rudy, and Halil for being you; Devora for being there; and Jeff and Rachel for being honest.

Thanks to Eli Segal, who generously shared his special powers with so many. To Rodney Carroll: There wouldn't be a book two without book one. To Kate Carr, who for some reason keeps hiring me—maybe the only questionable decision she ever makes. And to my Aunt Judy, a great believer in the power of books. Unfortunately, she isn't around to see this one, but I think she would have liked it.

Thanks so much to Richard Lena, Cecilia Chard, and Brattle Publishing for taking a chance on this series. I hope this is the start of a beautiful partnership. I'm not a good enough writer to express all my appreciation to Carol. Thank you for all your patience, perseverance, and everything else you did to make this project happen.

Finally, there's Dixie. I could write another book about how Dixie is the coolest person in the world and how lucky I am to share my life with her. If I did, it would be called "Perfect to Me," because that's what she is.

Part I

The Connection

What's an Akaway?

"Freeze," said Grammy, in the spirited tone that she saved for particularly important discoveries. She took an eagle's feather out of her backpack and pointed to an imprint in the snow. It was the first snow of the season, which everyone knows is the best time to search for fresh tracks.

"Oh, my sweet cousin from Kalamazoo with double chocolate mud brownies and pulled pork sandwiches," Grammy said. "Do you know what this is?"

"An animal track," said Brody Boondoggle.

"Nope, it's an animal track," answered Grammy.

Brody had learned recently not to say things like, "That's what I said," when Grammy didn't hear him properly, because she wouldn't hear that either.

For some reason, Grammy's senses hadn't been as sharp lately. Two months ago, she lost feeling in her right hand. Brody noticed when she kept poking herself with a pin while sewing patches on his favorite pair of jeans. Just last month, she lost the ability to see colors. Brody noticed when she unknowingly kept eating the blue M&M's, the ones she swore to boycott because she believed eating them made her feel blue. And now, Grammy was losing her hearing. It was almost completely gone in her left ear and it was starting to fade in the right.

"And do you know what kind of animal track?" Grammy asked. This time, she didn't even wait for an answer. "It's an Akaway," she said. "An Akaway."

"What's an Akaway?" asked Brody.

"Oh, about 50 pounds," said Grammy. "Maybe a little more after a big meal. But that's not important now."

Brody paused for a second, looked up to the sky, shook his head slightly back and forth, then slowly maneuvered over to Grammy's right side. He spoke slowly and clearly.

"I said, 'What is an Akaway?'"

"Oh," chuckled Grammy. "Yes. An Akaway is one of the rarest creatures in the universe." She moved closer and whispered, "And one of the most important. Nobody's ever seen one before."

Then how does she know what its footprints look like? Brody thought to himself. But before he could ask Grammy directly, she turned to him and shouted, "Let's go!"

In a flash, Grammy was off. Now Grammy might be a grandmother, and she might be losing her vision, her hearing, and her sense of touch, but she knew her way around these woods and she could run like a deer. Well, maybe a slightly older deer, with a little arthritis in her knees, who had just quit smoking a few years ago, and loved a decadent treat called Danish pastry. But the point was, she could cruise when she wanted to, and right now she was jumping over logs, ducking under branches, and busting through snowbanks. Brody's long legs and arms were pumping furiously, and he was still falling behind.

Finally she stopped abruptly, allowing Brody to catch up.

As he leaned over with his hands on his knees, trying

to catch his breath, everything Brody ever knew about animals suddenly flashed through his mind. And there was plenty to flash, because if there was one thing Brody knew, it was animals. Reptiles and mammals, birds and insects, amphibians, and fish. Even those tiny little bacteria on the underside of rocks at the bottom of the ocean, which are really only half animal, half plant; but that was close enough for Brody, so he knew about plankton as well.

But he never even dreamed of an Akaway.

"Do you see it?" asked Grammy. She pointed through the woods to a huge rock next to the snow-covered lake. "Please tell me you see it."

And at that point Brody understood how Grammy identified the footprints. Because even though he had no idea what an Akaway was, he knew for certain he was staring at one right now.

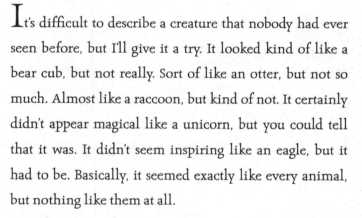

The Voice

It's difficult to describe a creature that nobody had ever seen before, but I'll give it a try. It looked kind of like a bear cub, but not really. Sort of like an otter, but not so much. Almost like a raccoon, but kind of not. It certainly didn't appear magical like a unicorn, but you could tell that it was. It didn't seem inspiring like an eagle, but it had to be. Basically, it seemed exactly like every animal, but nothing like them at all.

"That's an Akaway," said Grammy. "And, oh my monkey's uncle on Saturn with a green onion Philly cheesesteak and sweet potato fries, this one is an albino. It's the only one of its kind."

"How can you tell?" asked Brody.

"Oh, sweetie, they smell with their noses, just like you and me," said Grammy. "But I really don't see how that's important right now."

Again, Brody repositioned himself and repeated his question.

"I said, 'How can you tell?' not 'How do they smell?'" he said slowly.

"Oh," chuckled Grammy. "That would make more sense. The only difference is their eyes. Their eyes are pink. Take a close look."

At the same moment Brody cleared his long, black hair off his face to look the Akaway right in the eyes, the Akaway picked up its head and did the same thing to Brody. As the two animals stared at each other for what seemed like minutes, Brody felt something strange inside. A voice, calling him closer.

"Can I pet her?" Brody asked, raising his voice so Grammy could hear. And, of course, Grammy said, "Yes."

Brody confidently walked up to the Akaway as if it were a pet he had raised since birth. It seemed more like floating, but 11-year-olds can't float, so we'll say he was walking. The Akaway didn't move; instead, its ears went forward, its tail curled up, and it tilted its head just enough to make Brody sure he was welcome to come closer.

And then. . . . "Ow!" yelled Brody, as he fell to the ground, holding his face in his hands. "That thing bit me."

In a flash, the Akaway was gone.

Changes

Brody Boondoggle was completely unaware that, at that moment, a very important connection was being made, meaning the bite from the Akaway was initiating a subtle, yet powerful, transformation deep inside his soul. And he certainly had no idea that soon this new energy inside him would unite his mind and his body so completely that not only would he know all about animals, but he could act like them as well.

Instead, Brody was completely focused on how the fresh white snow on the ground directly under his face was slowly changing to red, drop by drop, like paint dripping on a canvas.

"It's beautiful," said Grammy, referring to the image in the snow. "What do you call it?"

"Grammy!" Brody cried so loudly that there was no doubt she could hear. "That's not funny. Didn't you see that crazy animal just bite me?"

"Yeah, that was pretty interesting," said Grammy. "I wonder why she did that?"

"It's your fault," cried Brody. "That's why."

"You approached an unknown creature and it bit you," responded Grammy. "I really don't see how I'm involved."

"You told me it was okay. That's how you're involved," countered Brody.

"Oh, I don't think so," responded Grammy. "You asked, 'Can I pet it?' and I said, 'Yes.' That didn't mean it wasn't going to bite you. I assumed you knew what you were doing."

"How would I know what I was doing?" yelled Brody in astonishment. "I'd never even heard of an Akaway until five minutes ago."

"Then why would you just go up to it like that and try to pet it?" asked Grammy.

"Because you said it was magical," Brody screamed in frustration.

As always, Grammy was calm. "Oh, I'm quite sure that it is," said Grammy. "Especially an albino. It's the most magical of all."

"Then why did it attack me?" asked Brody.

"You really have to stop saying that," cautioned Grammy. "Word might get out, and pretty soon everyone will think the albino Akaway is a dangerous creature."

"But it is a dangerous creature."

"Oh, I'm quite sure that it's not," said Grammy. "Maybe you're a dangerous creature."

"Why do you always have to take the magical creature's side?" said Brody in his last attempt to win the argument. But, as usual, Brody knew he wouldn't, so he let out a surrendering sigh and plopped down on the snow. Grammy sat down next to him and handed him a snowball, which he instinctively put over his bloody eyebrow.

"Grammy," Brody said thoughtfully, breaking a few moments of silence. "If I tell you something, you promise you won't think I'm crazy?"

"Oh, sweetheart, I don't think you're lazy," Grammy said. "You just don't apply yourself sometimes. But one day, you'll figure it out."

"Crazy," Brody said, raising his voice. Once again, he methodically repositioned himself on Grammy's other side, a movement that was becoming a habit lately. "I don't want you to think I'm crazy," he repeated.

"Oh," chuckled Grammy. "Crazy. That's a different story. Of course you're crazy. We're all a little crazy. I couldn't imagine going through life without being a little crazy."

I don't know about that, Brody thought.

"Still," he continued. "This is gonna sound strange, but here goes." There was a short pause, and then, "The Akaway talked to me."

"That's perfect," Grammy said.

"But how? Why?" asked Brody.

"Those are questions I can't answer," said Grammy. "But I can tell you this: Everything happens for a reason."

"So what's the reason?" asked Brody.

"I have no idea," responded Grammy.

"But you said everything happens for a reason."

"It does," said Grammy.

"But that's what I'm trying to tell you," said Brody. "I heard a voice. Telling me to move closer. It wanted me right there next to it. I can't explain it. Do you believe me?"

"Oh, sweetie, it doesn't matter what I believe. Truth is not determined by what other people think. It comes from what you feel in your heart."

As usual, Brody was not interested in Grammy's philosophical slant on a simple question. But he also knew how this conversation would end if he tried to argue, so he didn't.

A moment passed before he asked quietly, "Do you think we'll ever see the Akaway again?"

Grammy stared straight ahead, so Brody raised his voice just a little.

"I said, 'Do you think we'll ever see the Akaway again?'"

"I heard you, sweetie," Grammy said, and then she pointed to the lake.

Brody and Grammy spent their next magical

moments together watching the Akaway sprint and slide back and forth on the newly frozen lake, like a baby penguin just discovering the powers of ice, or a baseball player sliding into third base, or a magical creature who knows it doesn't have much time left.

In the Game

"What'd it look like? Where'd it come from? Why's it here?" blurted Brody's best friend, Rudy, from the other end of the phone. These were the same questions Brody had about the Akaway, which made sense because Brody and Rudy seemed to be connected that way.

Sure, Brody was tall and Rudy was short. Brody had dark hair. Rudy's was light. Brody's favorite sport was basketball, while Rudy's was lying in bed until 10 o'clock in the morning. But they were both smart and funny—and just a little dark inside. And they each accepted the other for exactly who they were, which is the best thing a best friend can do. They even shared the same birthday.

"Well, do you at least remember where you saw it?" Rudy finally asked when Brody couldn't answer any of his other questions. And Brody ended the conversation by revealing the exact location.

Brody's big brother, Jake, wasn't nearly as enthusiastic. "Yeah, and I'm a cheeky monkey," said Jake sarcastically, which also made sense because the two brothers didn't seem to be connected at all.

Brody loved spending time with Grammy, especially right around his birthday when they would walk in the woods by the lake near the cottage where Grammy lived. The woods contained endless trails, each leading to its own adventure, and it was on these walks that Brody and Grammy talked about animals and magic and all the endless possibilities in the world.

Jake clearly didn't believe in all that stuff. And since everyone knows that nothing takes the magic out of a walk more than someone who doesn't believe, Grammy never insisted that Jake come along, although Brody secretly hoped that she would. Over time, the two brothers just drifted further and further apart. It got to the point where Jake wasn't even invited on the walks, and Brody stopped caring—or at least he pretended to.

"But I'm telling the truth," insisted Brody. "It was incredible."

"I'll tell you what's incredible," said Jake, holding up a sleek and stylish contraption. "This video game. It fits in the palm of my hand. I can take it with me at all times. And the graphics—it's like I'm actually in the game. Do you know how cool it is to be in a video game?" Then he flipped it over. "It's even got a shiny metallic coating on the back that I can use as a mirror."

Brody waited appropriately for Jake to sneak a peak in the "mirror" to make sure his wavy hair was still purposefully messed up in all the right places. Then, Brody shot back, "Yeah, well it's not cooler than an Akaway."

"Maybe not," said Jake. "But at least it's real."

"So's an Akaway," argued Brody.

Jake just ignored him, which of course made Brody even angrier.

Brody pointed to a spot just above the outside corner of his left eye. "If it's not real, how'd I get this?"

This time, Jake did glance up, but only for a second to inspect the area in question. "I don't see anything," he said.

"What are you talking about?" cried Brody, still pointing. "The Akaway bit me."

"Sounds like a dangerous creature," said Jake.

He shoved the mirror side of his video game in Brody's face. "But there's nothing there. Check it out for yourself."

Brody did. He could see the bite clearly in the mirror—a cut above his left eye. It was even bleeding just a little. "Very funny, Jake," he said, gently tapping the cut. "Ask Grammy. She saw the Akaway. She'll tell you it's real."

Jake put down his game and looked up. "Listen to me carefully," he said. "Just because Grammy says it doesn't make it true. And besides, I'm not like you. I don't believe what other people tell me. My motto is: 'Why have a motto when you can have a slogan?' And my slogan is: 'I believe it when I see it.'"

At that moment, a soft voice made its way down the stairs into the living room. It was Grammy asking Jake very nicely to come up and see her. Jake ran upstairs, and that's when Grammy filled him in on a secret she'd been keeping for a few months now. It was an important secret that she didn't want to share, but now, she knew she had to.

It seems Grammy wasn't doing so well. She tried to

hide it from Brody, but this last hike had taken a lot out of her. She didn't know why or exactly what the problem was, but she was getting worse and would need some time to get better.

"The next few weeks leading up to Brody's birthday might be a little tough on your brother, because this is the time we're usually off on our adventures," she reminded Jake. "But I don't have the strength for our usual adventures right now."

She looked up at Jake. "I need you to take my place with Brody, even if you don't believe a word he says. Can you do that for me?"

"Can't he just hang out with Rudy?" Jake suggested.

But Jake knew that there was something about Rudy that Grammy never truly trusted, so he wasn't surprised when she responded by saying, "This is important. That's why I'm asking you."

Jake was definitely not perfect. Yes, he purposely chewed too loud because he knew it bothered Brody. And there were definitely times when he chose to criticize Brody when he could have encouraged him. And there was no doubt that he often dismissed Brody's stories about magical creatures when he could have embraced them. But deep down, Jake was a good big brother. And, therefore, he knew full well that this was one of those moments when his little brother needed him.

So he kissed Grammy on the cheek and whispered, "I promise." And although he really had no idea what that promise would lead to, he did know where to start.

"Okay, Brody," said Jake, wiping his eyes as he returned from upstairs. "This Akaway you're babbling about. Let's see it."

Drifting Together

It was the first time in a long time that Jake and Brody were outside together, but today they worked as a team, navigating trails, tracking footprints, and climbing hills. They talked very little, except to say things like, "Try to stay in my footprints," or "Do you think I can hit that tree with a snowball?" or "If you could be a chicken or a butt, which would you be?" And at the end of a long, tough journey, all the work was worth it. They were alone, squatting next to the still newly frozen lake, being treated to one of the rarest of all sights.

"What do you say about that?" said Brody, staring at the Akaway in awe. "Now do you believe me?"

"Why would I?" replied Jake. "There's nothing there."

"Yes, there is."

"No, there isn't."

The debate went back and forth as if Brody might eventually convince Jake that the Akaway was actually there, or Jake might actually convince Brody that it wasn't. But the truth was, they were both telling the truth.

Here's how: Like all animals, including you and me, Akaways have defense mechanisms, which are basically special powers we all use when we feel threatened. The Malaysian ant actually explodes when a predator gets close, spraying poison on its enemy. Unfortunately, it's not around to enjoy the moment. The Pacific hagfish oozes a disgusting, slimy substance when it's attacked. Its prey is trapped in this slime and usually dies.

As for the Akaway, it can become invisible. So if you're someone trying to harm it, you can't see it. And even if you're someone who just doesn't believe, like Jake, you can't see it either.

"Yes, there is."

"No, there isn't."

"Yes, there is."

"No, there isn't."

This could have gone on for hours if someone hadn't interrupted.

"What are you guys arguing about?" someone interrupted.

He was actually an unimposing man, meaning he wasn't particularly big or particularly small. The man wore a thick rope like a sash around his shoulder, carried a brown leather satchel, and clung to what seemed like a standard hunting rifle, which made sense because this guy could not have looked more like a hunter if he tried. All except for the gray-and-black speckled pig that stood next to his right leg. Its tag read: Gizmo.

"Is there something out there?" the hunter asked.

"It's an Akaway," said Brody.

"What's an Akaway?" asked the hunter.

"Oh, about 50 pounds," Brody responded with a chuckle. The hunter and Jake smiled, too.

"It's a magical creature," Brody continued.

"Well, that's a creature I'd like to see. Where is it?" said the hunter, sticking his neck out and squinting. "'Cuz I don't see a thing."

A strange feeling came over Jake as he watched the hunter and then made eye contact with Gizmo—like a soft warning from deep inside that something didn't seem right.

The hunter slid his rifle around his shoulder, pointed it in the direction Brody had indicated, and peered through the scope.

"Hey," yelled Brody, darting to his right so that he was between the rifle and the Akaway. "What do you think you're doing with that gun?"

"Relax there, little man," said the hunter, pushing Brody out of the way. "This isn't a real gun. Check it out. I invented it myself."

The hunter aimed the "fake" gun at a nearby rock and pulled the trigger.

"Zzzzzzz-pow."

Brody's and Jake's eyes widened as a ray of light shot out of the gun, hit the rock, and then engulfed it in what seemed like a glowing, yellow cocoon.

"See that?" said the hunter with pride. "This thing couldn't hurt a fly. Just makes everything easier to see—like a highlighter." Then he added, "Things that are actually there, that is."

"Oh, it's there," said Brody, again pointing to the lake where the Akaway was currently sitting, as if deeply interested in the interaction.

"Okay, prove it," challenged the hunter. He reached into his satchel and pulled out what seemed like a regular pair of sunglasses. "Here," he said, handing the glasses to Brody. "Put them on. This is going to be really cool."

"Another one of your inventions?" asked Jake cautiously.

"I've been working on these for a while," said the hunter. He explained that the glasses were connected to the site of the laser, meaning whatever Brody saw through the glasses, the hunter could see in the laser.

"All you have to do is stare at that albino little bugger," said the hunter. "And I'll be able to see it once and for all. And then I'll believe you."

That sounded good to Brody, who placed the sunglasses on his face. The hunter peered through the site of his laser, which seemed to magically follow the same path as Brody's eyes.

As Jake watched, that soft warning deep inside his belly got louder. *How did the hunter know the Akaway was albino?* Jake quickly turned back to look at the rock. It was still glowing, but it seemed different. Smaller. Shriveled up like a prune.

"There," said Brody proudly, staring at the Akaway. "It's right there. You can't miss it."

"Perfect," said the hunter, his laser automatically moving just slightly down and to the right.

And even though Jake felt a little awkward protecting a creature that he still didn't believe existed, he knew what the hunter was going to do next. So he lunged for the laser.

"Zzzzzzz-pow."

Unfortunately, he was too late.

Pig Drool

Now it was the Akaway that was swallowed by the yellow, glowing light of the laser, and immediately Brody knew something was very wrong. Deep down in his soul, he could feel the Akaway getting weaker and weaker. As if its spirit was being sucked right out of its body.

"What have you done?" Brody yelled, ripping the sunglasses from his face.

"You tell me," replied the hunter, who still couldn't see the Akaway.

Brody stared out at the newly frozen lake. But only for a second because then he bolted, running toward the Akaway with all his might but getting absolutely nowhere.

"Where on earth do you think you're going, little man?" said the hunter, holding Brody securely with his left hand, the laser still beaming in his right.

"Let me go," Brody demanded. "Let me go. I have to help her."

"You can't go out there," said the hunter. "You'll fall right through that ice. And I, for one, won't be sending Gizmo out to save you."

Brody struggled, but he couldn't break free of the hunter's grip. Brody looked out to see more and more of the Akaway's spirit being sucked from her body.

"Jake," he pleaded. "She's dying. I can save her. I know you can't see her, but you gotta believe me."

"No, you don't," countered the hunter. "Listen," he said in a tone that implied some respect for Jake's judgment. "You seem like a reasonable young man. You need to trust your instincts. You need to be smart. And letting this maniac run out on that lake after a creature that doesn't exist is not smart. You know just as well as I do, there's no such thing as an Akaway."

The hunter was right, and Jake knew it. Helping Brody might not have been the smartest thing to do. But trusting his instincts was. And right now, Jake's instincts were telling him exactly what to do.

"Take your hands off my brother," he ordered, staring the hunter right in the eye.

But the hunter just stood there. He wasn't going to move. So Jake did, charging directly at him. Jake lunged his shoulder into the hunter's left kneecap, creating just enough of an impact to cause the hunter to release Brody before crumbling to the ground.

"Run!" yelled Jake.

But just as Jake was about to dive back on the hunter, Gizmo did what any good sidekick would do: he got in the way. And that fat little pig was fast. At first contact, Jake stumbled backwards but quickly regained his balance. He pointed two fingers directly at his eyes, then to Gizmo. "You're going down," he said. And Gizmo grunted back in a tone that basically meant, "Bring it on."

In seconds, it was now Jake who was pinned to the ground, Gizmo seemingly mocking Jake, while drooling all over his face—big, thick, disgusting, pig drool.

"You're nothing but a big piece of bacon," yelled Jake, thrusting Gizmo to the side and rolling on top. "If I liked lettuce and tomato, I'd eat you in a big BLT."

"Oink, oink, oink, oink, oink, oink," replied Gizmo, which probably meant something like, "That is so cliché, surely you can think of something more poetic than that." And Gizmo shifted his weight in just the right way, causing Jake to fall to the side. The battle continued. One second, Gizmo was on top; the next second, it was Jake who seemed to be in control. Neither would give up or give in.

In the confusion, Brody took off toward the lake, but before he could get away, the hunter lunged for his ankle and grabbed hold. Brody's heart raced, knowing Jake could no longer help him because he was in the middle of an intense wrestling match with a pig named Gizmo.

Brody struggled with all his might, but it was no use.

This guy is as big as a caribou, thought Brody. *I'd have to be as strong as a rhinoceros beetle to break free.*

And that's when Brody Boondoggle realized he had special powers.

Rhinoceros Beetle

A rhinoceros beetle can lift 850 times its own weight—a piece of information that would ordinarily have no effect on Brody. But now, thanks to the bite of the Akaway, things for Brody would never be ordinary again. Now, his mind and body were so fully in tune that just thinking of a rhinoceros beetle suddenly made him feel stronger. And then the hunter's grip weakened. It was only slightly, but the hunter and Brody both sensed it. *A rhinoceros beetle*, Brody thought. And then he focused. *I'm a rhinoceros beetle. I'm a rhinoceros beetle.*

Adrenaline pumped through his body, and Brody Boondoggle knew that in just another moment, he would be strong enough to escape the grip of the hunter. And that's exactly what happened.

His first instinct was to help his brother, but Jake quickly waved him off.

"Go," he ordered, Gizmo firmly planted on his stomach. The hunter popped to his feet and chased Brody to the edge of the lake. But he stopped abruptly when his boot went through the first sheet of ice.

"Gizmo, after him," the hunter ordered. Immediately, Gizmo darted for the lake, but the pig only made it a few feet farther than the hunter before he, too, felt the ice crack and wisely scampered back to shore. Jake watched from his belly and listened closely as the hunter shrieked, "Come back here, little man. You can't save her, you know. It's too late."

But Brody kept going.

"He's crazy," said the hunter in disgust. He looked back at Jake. "You're both crazy."

Jake pulled himself up and ran past the hunter to the edge of the lake. Brody was ten feet past the point where Gizmo had already cracked the ice, creeping inch by inch farther and farther away from safety.

Crack.

Brody froze. Unfortunately, the ice didn't—at least not all the way through.

Another inch and another...crack. This crack was bigger. Brody wasn't going to make it.

"Give me your rope," Jake barked to the hunter. He stuck out his hand but kept his eyes focused on Brody. There was no rope. "Give me your rope," Jake repeated. Now he was yelling. But still his hand was empty. He turned his head with fury and started to repeat himself for a third time, but there was no one there to listen.

The hunter and Gizmo were gone. If he had had time to scan the area, Jake might have seen them duck behind a nearby tree, watching everything that would happen next, but Jake's attention shifted immediately back to the lake.

"You gotta come back," Jake yelled, and Brody knew that it was the only smart decision. And Brody was going to do it too. Until he heard this: *Trust your instincts.* It was that little voice again.

Brody Boondoggle only had a split second to decide if he was going to head back to safety or listen to this new voice.

Trust your instincts.

He heard it again. And Brody listened. He focused as hard as he could, trying to weigh less than an ordinary hand towel.

Think, he said to himself. *I have to be light.*

He took a few more steps. Another crack. And this crack was even larger than the one before. He looked down. The lake seemed like a spider's web. A central crack in the middle with slivers darting out in all directions.

What's the lightest animal you can think of?

"Plankton," Brody blurted. "That's it. I'm plankton. I'm plankton."

We have already learned that 11-year-old boys can't float, but if you asked Jake, he'd swear that at that moment, when Brody concentrated on being plankton, he practically floated across the lake. Jake wouldn't have believed it if he hadn't seen it with his own eyes. And with every step, Brody felt himself getting lighter and lighter, more and more confident that he actually was plankton, or at least as light as plankton.

The Akaway seemed peaceful when Brody finally came to its rescue.

"I'm here," whispered Brody. He removed his heavy winter coat, transforming it into a warm, supportive blanket. "It's okay." Then he carried the jacket and the Akaway safely back to shore, where the creature that only Brody could see opened its eyes and tilted its head just as it had done right before it struck Brody above the eye. Brody felt the spot. It was still bleeding, but just barely. He shrugged and smiled.

But the smile slowly faded when Brody looked into the eyes of the Akaway. The pink was fading, and somehow Brody knew exactly what that meant. Then the Akaway lay down and closed its eyes for what might or might not have been the last time.

Own Little
Universe

As Brody sat in the snow with Jake and the Akaway, thinking of all the chaos and all the craziness of the current situation, he actually smiled, because at that point, he remembered the one person who would know exactly what to do when you bring a magical creature to her house and explain that it was just lasered by a hunter, with the help of a pig named Gizmo.

"Come on, Jake, help me carry her," Brody said. He scampered to his feet and grabbed one end of the jacket on which the Akaway lay. "We're going to Grammy's."

Without uttering a word of protest, Jake complied, which means he grabbed the other half of the jacket, even though he still didn't see the Akaway or even feel it as he walked side by side with Brody back the way they had come. They talked very little, except to say things like, "Watch out for that branch," or "What do you think happened to that hunter?" or "I used to think that cows peed milk."

There were twisted ankles and scraped faces, and their boots were so soaked that by the midpoint of the crossing they could hear a rhythmical "squish" with every step. But when Brody and Jake finally exited the trail by the railroad track, maneuvered the Akaway over the wooden fence, and turned onto the path that led directly to Grammy's, Brody had hope that everything might be okay.

Grammy's house had a way of making him feel that way. She lived in a small, antiquated, or old-fashioned, cottage that was always warm, thanks to an antique wood-burning stove in the middle of the living room. The colors in the house were vivid, meaning they were bright and alive, and it made anyone inside feel that way as well.

The walls were lined with shelves, stuffed with all kinds of mythical books about things most people didn't believe. Each room was its own little universe, sharing its own stories about how the world was, is, and should be. All you had to do was listen.

"Grammy, please," cried Brody after storming through the front door and calling loud enough for Grammy to hear. "I think she's dying."

"Oh my, sweet sister of Jupiter and all that tastes good with turkey gravy and corned beef hash," Grammy whispered to the heavens. And although she tried to appear calm, the quiver in her voice betrayed her.

Jake slowly retreated to the corner of the room, not knowing what to make of Grammy's profound reaction to a creature that didn't exist. But Brody stayed, watched, and waited as Grammy calmed herself with five deep breaths— in through her nose, out through her mouth—then brought her hands above her head and down to her sides.

"Okay," she said, her voice now steady. "Let's get her comfortable."

Supporting the bottom of the jacket, she helped Brody carry the Akaway into the living room and gently laid it next to the wood-burning stove. There she bent down on one knee. Brody quickly followed, watching and hoping intently. Looking purposefully at the Akaway, Grammy scanned it up and down with her eyes before doing the same with her hands. Then she bent over, placing her ear on the Akaway's chest. She closed her eyes for what seemed like hours. Finally, she looked up and nodded her head.

"Yes," Grammy said softly, looking directly at Brody. "She's dying."

An African Elephant and a Fire Ant

Brody Boondoggle's body hit the ground like a beehive falling from a tree, which is pretty standard when your emotions get so intense and so overwhelming that it's too much to handle for an 11-year-old boy who has just rescued an Akaway. And when that happens, your mind turns off, your body shuts down, and the weight of the world wins, if only for a while.

THUD.

As a rule, you should probably worry at least a little when any child faints, but in this case, Grammy didn't seem overly concerned.

"He'll be fine," Grammy whispered to Jake.

Even with all her aches and pains, she hoisted Brody's legs into the air. "Do you think you can help me carry him to my bed?"

Jake grabbed Brody's shoulders, and together Grammy and Jake moved Brody up the stairs, bumping his head against the railing and stairs only a few times along the way. His hips and ankles took a few hits as well.

"Those are probably good for him," Grammy joked. "Toughen the kid up a little bit." And Jake smiled. Then they laid him down peacefully on Grammy's water bed, which everyone knows is the best kind of bed for having extraordinary dreams.

"Sleep well," Grammy whispered, and she gave Brody a kiss on the forehead. She then backed away from the bed, and Jake followed her down to the living room, where there was a lengthy, awkward silence as they stood beside the jacket that either did or did not contain the Akaway, depending on what you believed. And it was that silence that illustrated everything you needed to know about the relationship between Grammy and her oldest grandson, who were as different as an African elephant and a fire ant.

The funny thing was, down deep, Jake wished he could

believe in all the things Grammy just accepted as fact. He wanted to believe that there was actually a sixth sense we all had that connected everything in the universe, but he just couldn't feel it. He wanted to believe that everyone had a third eye that provided the ability to see things such as auras, which Grammy believed was the energy that surrounded all of us, but he just couldn't see it. He wanted to believe in spirits, and fantasy, and all the other unexplained types of magic that could lead to great adventures. But even at 13 years old, Jake was a reasonable person, and reasonable people just didn't believe in that kind of stuff, even if they really wanted to.

Grammy asked Jake to help carry the jacket that supposedly contained the Akaway onto the water bed, so that's what he did. They placed the jacket peacefully next to Brody, which led to a few more awkward silences. Finally, they decided it was probably best to just go to sleep.

Jake was mentally and physically exhausted, and as he crawled into his sleeping bag—Grammy already asleep on the couch—he would have loved to simply close his eyes and start dreaming of video games. But no matter how hard he tried, he couldn't. Grammy was already snoring like a wounded cow.

"Mooooooooaaaaaaah, Mooooooooaaaaaaah."

And if you've ever been kept awake by snoring—the kind of snoring that is so offensive, no amount of earplugs in your ears or pillows over your head will help—you know that after a while you'll do almost anything to make it stop, even if the snorer isn't feeling so well.

So with Brody and the Akaway sleeping side-by-side upstairs on the water bed, Jake slipped out of his sleeping bag and quietly, yet aggressively, began pummeling Grammy with pillows.

"Mooooooooaaaaaaah, Mooooooooaaaaaaah."

When that didn't work, he rocked her with all his might to flip her over on her stomach. Held her nose for five seconds. Stuffed cotton balls up her nose. Placed a golf ball between her shoulder blades.

"Mooooooooaaaaaaah, Mooooooooaaaaaaah."

Nothing worked, so Jake was forced to move to the last line of defense against the loud snoring. He started looking for another place to sleep, which led him on an exploration of all the rooms in Grammy's house that until now he barely even knew existed.

The Icequarium

The cloud-covered tapestry that acted as a door to the room next to Grammy's kitchen caught Jake's attention. There was a small hole in one of the clouds that allowed a beam of light to shine through. Jake's eyes were heavy and his energy was low, but he followed that beam to a large book about the size of a pizza box with strange, colorful images on the cover.

He pulled the book from the shelf and gently placed it on a desk that Grammy and Brody had purchased at a garage sale because they were sure it had been made in medieval times and probably contained some magic. Then, with what seemed like his last ounce of energy, Jake forced himself to flip open the book, and he began to read.

Jake could feel the energy slowly but steadily returning to his body as he studied each page. He felt stronger still when he grabbed another book and read that one as well. One book led him to another and then another and another. His mind was working in ways he never dreamed of. Maybe he was dreaming. But either way, slowly Jake was starting to form a perfectly beautiful scenario of exactly what could be happening to his brother and why. When he consumed all the books in the room that had anything to do with the magical creatures, he went to another room down the hall and devoured those books as well.

When there were no more books to read, he investigated other rooms, digging through drawers, flipping through papers, and studying pictures. He took copious notes, which means he wrote down interesting themes, reoccurring names, and anything that seemed important. He kept his notes in a small black book, which fit easily in the back pocket of his favorite jeans. Just like his video game.

As the sun started to rise, Jake finished his investigation of all the rooms in Grammy's house, except one.

Grammy's bedroom was relatively bare and ordinary, especially for a home that seemed to hold so many secrets. The jacket that may or may not have contained the Akaway, depending on who was looking, still lay next to Brody in the middle of Grammy's water bed. Beside the bed there was a closet filled to the top with sweaters and pants and things Jake didn't really care to examine.

The room was dark, except for a single flea-market lamp on a table next to the bed that barely offered enough glow to see the array of pictures covering the walls. Jake strolled around the room carefully examining them all— amused by the odd combinations, like a crab in a hot tub, an octopus climbing a tree, or a fish performing surgery.

Across the room from the bed was a single dresser that Grammy had made and decorated herself. Without really knowing why, Jake opened the top drawer to find Grammy's collection of socks. Warm socks for the winter, coupled into unmatched pairs and rolled into balls. All in pairs except for one single sock, a lumpy one, which lay alone, across the side of the drawer.

Jake thought for a second and cautiously scanned the

room to make sure Brody and the empty coat were still asleep. Convinced it was safe, he carefully reached down into the sock and pulled out what seemed like six ordinary gray rocks about the size and shape of silver dollars. But when Jake turned to the light for a closer look, he noticed that each rock had a thin hole just inside the edge and a small symbol in the middle—like a subtle imprint.

"They're magic."

The soft-crackling voice coming from the doorway startled Jake, and he turned quickly to see Grammy. He seemed concerned as he peered at Grammy, whose hands were mysteriously behind her back. But the concern quickly turned to delight when Grammy revealed what she was hiding.

It was a big glass bowl—a fishbowl, actually. Only instead of water, pebbles, and plastic plants, it was filled with strawberry ice cream, pineapple, and pound cake, topped with chocolate truffles and whipped cream with a heaping spoonful of colored sprinkles—filled all the way to the top.

"You know what this is?" asked Grammy.

Jake immediately recognized the creation Grammy

saved for very special occasions, even if he'd never had one before.

"An Icequarium," he said.

"Nope, it's an Icequarium," said Grammy. She then brought her other hand out from behind her back: two spoons. "Time for breakfast," she said smiling.

Jake sat down on the bed next to Grammy, the waves from the water bed seeming to rock Brody and the Akaway deeper and deeper into sleep. Working together in silence for a short time, they finished almost half of the Icequarium before Jake got up and moved over to Grammy's good ear. He looked at the jacket and then asked just loud enough for Grammy to hear, "Why do you believe in all this stuff?"

"What stuff?" Grammy asked with a mouth full of pound cake.

"You know, magical stuff?"

Grammy swallowed and licked the spoon clean. "Well, that's an easy one," she said. "Because it's all around me. In all the little miracles in the world. The fact that we can all love and laugh and lollygag. That's all magic."

Jake smiled politely before clarifying. "That's not the

kind of magic I'm talking about."

"Oh, my love," said Grammy. "There is no other kind."

Jake took another big bite of ice cream. Maybe it was because he had just pulled his first all-nighter and was too tired to hold himself back. Maybe it was because he was inspired by all he had read. And maybe it was just the sugar from his breakfast, but he finally gathered up the courage to ask something he'd been wondering about for as long as he could remember.

"But what if you don't believe?" He paused for a second. "Does it mean there's something wrong with you?"

"Now why would you wonder about something like that?" Grammy said softly.

"You know, because I never really believed in this stuff like you and Brody. I never really fit in with you guys."

It took a lot for Grammy to willingly put down a half-finished Icequarium, but after giving it some thought, she took her hands off the bowl and shifted them to Jake's shoulders.

"Oh, my love, please don't ever worry about fitting in," she said. "Different is good. I can talk to you about what I see and feel and believe, and then you can tell me about the things you see and feel and believe. And that's the great gift we can give each other. That's the magic."

Jake nodded, a little embarrassed, a little confused, and a little reassured all at the same time.

"The stories in your books. The stuff about the magical creatures and spirit animals and these rocks," Jake said, showing the six rocks to Grammy. "You really think it's all real?"

"I think a better question is, 'Do you?'" asked Grammy.

Jake stared at the rocks. "I'd like to believe these rocks are magic," he said. "I'd like to believe they are the keys to a secret and powerful world. But realistically, it doesn't make sense. Rocks can't be magic."

When Jake tried to return the rocks to Grammy, she refused to take them, so he put them in his pocket. After a few more moments of eating and silence and gazing at the invisible Akaway, Jake spoke again.

"We're going to save her, you know."

Jake paused for a second, then repeated, "Save her, Grammy. We're going to save the last Akaway. Brody and me. That's what we're going to do together. Until his birthday. Until you get better. I figured it out."

"That would be a beautiful use of your time," Grammy said softly.

Jake noticed Grammy's eyes. They looked tired.

"You are going to get better," he said. "If we do this? Right, Grammy?"

Grammy just shrugged and smiled. "All this makes me better," she said.

And as the sun continued to rise, and Brody and the Akaway continued to sleep, Jake sat with Grammy, connected for the first time, discussing all the questions that lay in the mysteries that Jake now knew about. And, oh yeah, they polished off the Icequarium while they were at it.

Sarraka

Brody Boondoggle's body lay perfectly still, but his mind was racing in a million different directions, conjuring up incredible dreams that seemed so real that he actually woke up in a cold sweat, wondering why he couldn't extend his arm long enough to reach the key to the giant waterslide that led to the most beautifully peaceful place on earth. And why was there a pigeon on his shoulder doing the chicken dance?

He fell out of bed in a foggy haze and stumbled downstairs to find Jake and Grammy at the kitchen table playing Scrabble with alphabet pasta and eating deep-fried macaroni and cheese.

"What happened?" asked Brody, pointing out all the bumps and bruises on his body. "How long was I asleep?"

"Oh, you're not a creep," said Grammy. "Sure, sometimes you're not very nice and you can be downright mean when you're tired, but you have some very positive qualities as well."

Jake held up his fingers and mouthed the words, "Three days."

"I had the dream again," said Brody. "I reach my hand as far as I can down in that hole but I just can't get the key. Why can't I reach that key?"

Suddenly Brody froze as he remembered the events that led to his prolonged nap.

"The Akaway?" Brody blurted.

Grammy and Jake shared a glance, then Grammy headed to the counter as Jake steered Brody to the kitchen table and explained that Grammy had covered the Akaway in a special secret eucalyptus and seaweed ointment.

"She's hanging in there," said Grammy, handing each of them a mug of her famous Tropical Sunrise Smoothie—it was the fresh honey and vanilla soy milk that made it so good.

Brody took a sip. He swallowed and thought for a second. He took one more sip before asking the next logical question, even if he was terrified of the answer. "Is she going to survive?"

It was a question Jake was waiting for. "That's up to us," he answered.

"What do you mean?"

"I mean we can save her."

"How?" asked Brody with great anticipation, meaning he would have slept on the roof for a week if he thought it would save the Akaway.

"Simple," said Jake. "We have to open the portal to Sarraka."

Brody dipped his head and raised his eyebrows at the same time.

"Am I supposed to know what that means?" he asked, hoping that somehow he would.

Jake reached into his back pocket and pulled out the video game.

"Oops," he said. "Wrong pocket."

He then reached into his other back pocket and pulled out the black notebook that contained all his notes from the research he had done during the past three days. As he started flipping through the pages, he motioned for Brody to take another sip of his smoothie—he would need his strength. Jake finally stopped at a picture he had drawn of a creature that looked just like every other animal and nothing like them at all.

"Okay," he said, "Let's start at the beginning." He pointed to the picture. "This is an Akaway. It is a rare and magical creature."

"I think I know that," grunted Brody.

"I know you know that," said Jake. "But do you know why it's so rare and magical?"

Brody was silent.

"I didn't think so," said Jake. "It's rare and magical because it's the only creature in the universe that can connect kids to their spirit animals."

"What's a spirit animal?" asked Brody.

Jake put down his notebook and explained that, according to the legend, everyone is born with a spirit animal. "It's a gift that we each get, like a big birthday present, on the day we are born," he said. He went on to say that, according to the legend, once you're connected to your spirit animal, you have all the powers that your spirit animal possesses because it's a part of you. "Those are your special powers, and you can use them for the rest of your life."

"But you said, 'once you're connected,'" said Brody. "Does that mean you're not connected as soon as you're born?"

"That's exactly what it means," said Jake. "The only way to be connected is by the Akaway. That's why the Akaway is so important."

"So what if there is no Akaway?" asked Brody.

"Well," said Jake. "If the Akaway were ever extinct, children would no longer have a way to connect to their spirit animals. They would have no way to get their special powers. And the problem is, if you don't try to find your powers and develop them at an early age, you tend to get older, and then you tend to believe less in them, and then your special powers just slowly fade away."

Brody thought for a second, digesting what he had just heard. A moment later, he looked at Jake and asked, "Do you have a spirit animal?"

"Of course I do," snapped Jake defensively. "Weren't

you listening? We all do."

"What is it?"

"I don't know," said Jake. "I haven't been connected."

"How do you know?"

"I just know," Jake snapped again. "It's something you know."

There was another pause while Brody took a brief inventory of his insides, meaning he closed his eyes, took a breath, and searched deep down in his soul. A few seconds later, he opened his eyes and whispered, "I'm connected, aren't I?"

Jake nodded. "When that Akaway bit you, it chose you."

Brody wiped the cut over his left eye. It was still bleeding, just a little, although Jake couldn't see it. "If you believe in that kind of stuff," Jake continued. "And if you do, then it chose you as its spirit animal. Chose you to have all its powers. It doesn't happen often, but when it does, it happens for a reason."

"But why?"

"Maybe to save its life."

Strange Man and His Sidekick

A small seed of pride started blooming in Brody's belly, or maybe it was the power from the Akaway getting stronger. But either way, Brody felt ready to do whatever it took to open the portal to Sarraka and save the Akaway.

"Okay," he said. "Tell me everything I need to know."

And that's what Jake did. He described how the universe is made up of many different worlds. "Two of those worlds are the spirit animal world, otherwise known as Sarraka, and our world," Jake explained. "The Akaway is dying," he added, "because it's not getting enough energy from its home."

"Sarraka?" guessed Brody.

"Exactly," said Jake. "So, in order to get the Akaway the extra energy it needs to survive, we need to open the portal that connects Sarraka and our world. It's pretty much that simple."

"No problem," said Brody, ready to begin. "So where do we start?"

Jake slid his notebook to Brody. Even at first glance it was obvious who would know the exact location of the portal and probably anything else they needed to learn about saving the Akaway.

"Felonious Fish," Brody said aloud, repeating the name that was highlighted, bolded, and underlined more than any other.

"It says here that Felonious Fish used to be a leader in the spirit animal world," read Brody. "But he resigned his commission, became some sort of fish doctor, and has not been heard from since." Brody's eyes drifted to the ceiling. "I wonder why?"

"There's no need to cry," said Grammy. "You're kind of a little crybaby. But don't worry too much about it. I'm sure you'll grow out of it."

"Why do you think Felonious ended his work with

Sarraka?" restated Jake, who happened to be on the side of Grammy's good ear.

"That's a mystery," Grammy said.

"So is how we're going to find him," said Brody. "According to this, he's not real interested in being found."

"Maybe yes and maybe no," said Grammy, painfully rising from her chair.

Brody and Jake watched as Grammy left the room, then returned a few minutes later with the picture from her room of the fish performing surgery. She opened the silver picture frame and unfolded the contents hidden behind the picture to reveal a large piece of paper covered in images and sketches.

"Do you know what this is?" asked Grammy, carefully smoothing out the paper with her forearms.

"It's a map," said Brody.

"Nope, it's a map," said Grammy. Brody rolled his eyes. He was getting good at that. "But it's more than that," she added. "It's a map of the last known location for Felonious Fish."

"How'd you get it?" asked Brody, but Grammy didn't hear him.

As Jake slid the map across the table to get a better view, he didn't notice the eyes of a man and his sidekick peering through the kitchen window, noting everything they saw. And neither did Grammy. But Brody Boondoggle did.

During his three-day nap, Brody's special powers had morphed so completely with his genetics that he didn't have to concentrate on being a bat. He could just hear like one without even trying.

"Do you hear something?" he said, picking up his head.

"I don't hear anything," said Jake, and Grammy didn't even hear the question.

His instincts were so in tune with his surroundings and his sixth sense was feeling so right that he didn't have to concentrate on being a rat either. He could just smell like one at almost all times.

"Do you smell something?" he said, lifting his nose in the air to detect a smell he could have sworn he recognized from a few days before.

"Nothing," said Jake, and Grammy didn't even smell the question.

And he didn't have to concentrate on being a jumping spider, the creature that has maybe the best vision of any creature on earth. That's because Brody's third eye was developing so completely that he could see the energy all around him, and he knew something wasn't quite right.

Brody grabbed Jake by the shoulder and offered a wink in a way that Jake had never seen before.

"It must be nothing," said Brody, slyly, and Jake understood.

"I'm going to the bathroom," said Jake.

"I'm going to check on the Akaway," said Brody.

"We'll be right back," they said in unison, and before Grammy could ask, "Who's Jack, and why would you want to bite him?" they had slid their chairs back, put their slippers on, and together walked up the stairs. It was strange because two brothers who until recently could barely share a pizza without arguing were now magically sharing the exact same idea.

Spy Mode

When you're going into spy mode, you don't feel the cold, so Jake and Brody Boondoggle were not the least bit deterred by the strong winds and blowing snow that met them as they opened the window in Grammy's bedroom and maneuvered their way onto the roof. When you're in spy mode, you're not scared of heights, so they calmly crept along the gutters, staying as low as possible until they reached the area directly above the kitchen window. And if you're truly in spy mode, you're not afraid of what might be lurking, so, in perfect unison, they dropped to a push-up position and lowered themselves slowly down on their stomachs, inching just a little bit closer to the edge of the

62

roof until their heads hung over the gutter.

"I've almost got enough," said the unimposing man, peering through a telephoto lens. Attached to his belt was a pole with a net, three extra leashes, a big knife that looked like a machete, and what seemed like the kind of pepper spray a dogcatcher would use, which made sense because this guy could not have looked more like a dog-catcher if he tried. All except for the creature that stood next to him, the one dressed to look like a sheep, with a name tag that read Doodad.

Click, click, click, click, click, click, click.

"He's taking pictures of the map," whispered Brody.

Now, it was Jake's turn to motion to Brody by putting two fingers to his eyes, then to the dogcatcher. Brody smiled and nodded because they were once again sharing the same idea.

You don't need to be bitten by an Akaway to have the power to make snowballs, every kid has it. So in what seemed like no time, Jake had created a pile of snowballs that matched the pile that Brody was making. Jake's index finger went up first. "One," he mouthed. Then his middle finger. "Two." Finally, his ring finger.

"Attack!" he yelled.

When he did, the two intruders looked up just in time to catch two perfectly aimed snowballs right between the eyes. They stumbled back as the ambush continued.

Pow, one in the back.

Boom, right in the shoulder.

Smack, right in the sheep.

"Retreat!" yelled the dogcatcher, protecting his camera as the snowballs kept coming with the speed and accuracy of a camel's spit. As the dogcatcher and Doodad ran straight into the forest, Jake took a running start and jumped right off the roof into the snowbank below. He paused for a second, looked up at Brody and asked what every little brother is waiting for his big brother to ask: "Are you coming?"

Alligator Falls

Brody Boondoggle could feel the power of the Akaway pulsing through his veins. It might have seemed strange to be chanting, "I'm a rainbow trout," over and over, but Brody knew that these creatures had a special substance in their bodies that they used as a compass to help them navigate. So, with Jake close behind, Brody was using that special substance too. Together, Jake and Brody sprinted up the hill by the train tracks, scampered across the fallen tree trunk, and dashed around the bend by the abandoned chimney.

"There," Brody said, pointing to Doodad, who looked back at the same moment, revealing a set of menacing eyes that Jake could have sworn he recognized. Then the sheep lowered his head and rushed right for the bridge over Alligator Falls. The dogcatcher waited on the other side of the bridge, his smile lighting up the night as much as the beams from the moon. He was calm and composed, standing peacefully as he waited—of course it's easy to be peaceful when you're the one carrying the machete.

Doodad pumped those hairy legs as fast as he could, and even though Brody and Jake were gaining, they knew it would be too late. Because as soon as Doodad crossed the bridge, the dogcatcher lifted his left arm and, with two powerful strikes in a row, cut the ropes that held the bridge, exposing a 50-foot drop into the water, with rocks so sharp they could rip apart human flesh.

"Bah, Bah, Bah," yodeled Doodad with great pride, and Jake had a feeling he knew exactly what that meant.

Then the dogcatcher and Doodad vanished around the next turn, watching secretly from behind a tree as Jake and Brody stood just on the edge of the ledge where the bridge used to be.

For the third time that evening, Jake and Brody understood what the other was thinking without saying a word.

And even the dogcatcher looked on with admiration as the two brothers backed up slowly, step by step, because he knew exactly what they were going to try.

At first they started walking, then jogging, then sprinting faster and faster directly toward a bridge that was no longer there. Then, just before the ground ended and the air began, Brody reached over and grabbed Jake's hand, and together, they jumped.

Thump

Brody flew through the air, probably concentrating on being a flying squirrel, while Jake's heart was pumping furiously because he was concentrating on not being a dead duck.

Then, in the middle of the flight, Brody turned his head and saw something he never expected. His big brother was grinning from ear-to-ear just like a kid with a strong connection to his spirit animal. That made Brody smile too, and that connection triggered the magic.

Things instantly froze. Brody took a deep breath, like the one you would take if you were about to dive down a waterslide you could never get off. Milliseconds later, everything moved in super slow motion. As Brody and Jake floated through the air, Brody saw a sharp burst of light and then nothing. He heard no noise, other than a beating heart.

THUMP, thump, thump, thump.

The beat seemed to be coming from two places—from Brody's own chest and also from directly next to him.

THUMP, thump, thump, thump.

They were synchronized. They were rhythmic. They were perfect.

Brody shook his head quickly, trying to snap out of whatever trance he must have been in. But if what you are experiencing is real, then you can't snap out of it. And there was no denying that what Brody was feeling was real.

He peered over at the animal that was gracefully soaring next to him in slow motion. Brody could see its long, lean muscles expanding with every poetic lunge through the air. Brody knew this animal. It was slightly larger than a normal house cat with a reddish brown coat and black spots scattered throughout its short, soft fur.

Brody blinked his eyes quickly as if he was snapping a picture, and everything sped up again. When the two brothers landed safely on the other side of the bridge, Brody blinked, and there was Jake. He blinked again. Now the creature. One more blink and things went back to normal—briefly anyway.

Jake glanced at Brody for only a split second, as if to ask, "What just happened?" Brody was desperate to tell him, but there was no time. The dogcatcher and Doodad were getting away. So Brody just shrugged and smiled back quickly. Then they both sprang to their feet and started running.

Unfortunately, they didn't run for long. The dogcatcher was smart. He didn't think Brody and Jake would be able to make that jump. But he prepared, just in case they did. That's why he planted the wire. The wire triggered a rope, and the rope, which was now fastened securely around Jake and Brody's ankles, was blasting into the sky like a rocket ship. The next thing they knew, Brody and Jake were hanging upside down from the top branch of a Sitka spruce tree.

But the funny thing was Brody wasn't worried that he was swaying back and forth, high in the air, in the middle of the winter night. And Jake wasn't angry that the bad guys had just scampered away in victory. Instead, Brody calmly turned to Jake and asked, "You want to hear something really cool?"

Jake paused for a moment and then replied just as calmly, "You know something Brody? This would be a perfect time to hear something really cool."

"I saw your spirit animal," Brody revealed. "You're an ocelot."

Maybe Magic

The next morning, Jake and Brody Boondoggle stayed in bed just a little longer than usual. That's what happens when your mind and body need recharging after a late-night adventure that ends with an uncanny combination of complete failure and total success.

Brody and Jake had successfully wiggled out of the rope, maneuvered across the shaky branch, and climbed safely down to the ground. During the walk home, Brody explained all about Jake's spirit animal, particularly that an ocelot was a kind of small leopard that is known to fight to the death. That made Jake smile.

But even though Jake may have been connected to his

spirit animal, the dogcatcher and Doodad were connected to the map. So when Brody and Jake finally awoke, there was only one thing on their minds—finding Felonious Fish before the dogcatcher did.

In what seemed like no time, they were dressed and heading out the door again. Grammy kissed them both on their foreheads and handed Jake a backpack with all the necessary supplies for a day in which no one knew what to expect.

"Tell that fish I said hi," said Grammy.

"Oh, Grammy, sometimes I wish I could fly, too," responded Brody, wryly. "But you still have a lot of very special gifts. None really come to mind right now, but I'll think of something and get back to you."

Grammy and Jake glanced at each other and then back at Brody, whose face didn't seem big enough to hold his grin. The best part about grins is that many times, they lead to smiles, then actual laughter, and before long, Grammy, Jake, and Brody were experiencing the big, full, belly laughs that are known to extend lives, end wars, and fuel adventures that just might open the portal, save the Akaway, and bring balance back to the universe.

"I wish you could come with us," said Brody, when the laugh fest finally ended.

"I would just slow you down," said Grammy. "Besides, I need to stay here with the Akaway. She'll need someone to talk with while you're on your adventure. Exciting stories are good for the soul."

Brody nodded, and although he said nothing, he was more worried than ever. Jake watched Brody give Grammy another big hug, and this time he didn't let go.

"Wait right here," he told Brody.

Jake quickly disappeared into Grammy's workroom and returned moments later with two matching dark leather cords. He pulled two of the magic rocks from his pocket—the first had the paw print of the ocelot. Jake looked down and then squeezed the rock tightly. In that instant, he felt warm. He felt right.

The other rock had a strange but distinct print that seemed so familiar but yet so unknown. With Brody watching with anticipation and Grammy watching with admiration, Jake skillfully threaded the leather cords through the holes in the rocks and then pulled them tight to make sure they were straight.

"Here," he said, tossing Brody a necklace. "Consider it an early birthday present."

Brody examined his gift carefully. He placed it around his neck and then proudly watched Jake do the same.

"You just made magic," Brody said, a huge smile dominating his face.

It didn't take the heightened senses of an ocelot to see that, at that moment, Brody's spirit got a little stronger. Jake could see it, and it actually made him feel good. Maybe the necklace really was magic, because the warm feeling that engulfed his body helped him see something else. It was subtle at first, but then Jake was sure of it. He smiled back. There was a cut above the outside corner of Brody's left eye—and Jake could see it.

Wrong Place, Wrong Time

What Jake didn't see was Rudy, who was just about to knock when Jake came storming out the front door. The collision threw Rudy right off the porch, over the railing, and into the bushes.

"Are you okay?" asked Brody, who rushed over to help his best friend back to his feet.

"Sorry about that, Rudacious," added Jake. "Wrong place, wrong time."

"I hate when he calls me Rudacious," Rudy mumbled before clearing the snow out of his collar and turning his attention to Brody. "I was just wondering, do you want to come over to my house and hang out?"

"I wish I could," answered Brody, thoughtfully. "But I'm hanging out with my brother today."

Rudy shook his head vigorously, stunned by what he'd just heard. He motioned for Brody to come closer, then whispered so Jake couldn't hear. "Is this the same brother who punches you, kicks you, and starts fights with you for no reason?"

"Pretty much," Brody whispered back. "But we have something really important going on today." He quickly explained everything to Rudy, while Jake offered consistent reminders that there was no time to waste.

"That sounds important," said Rudy after he heard the whole story. "Can I come?"

"No, you can't," interjected Jake, who had waited long enough. "C'mon, Brody. We gotta go."

This was the time of the conversation when Brody usually told Jake to "be quiet," or to "mind your own beeswax," or asked, "How about a nice hot cup of shut-your-piehole?" It was Rudy's favorite part and the reason he often went out of his way to cause trouble between the two brothers. It wasn't hard. The littlest thing could start a fight, and when it did, Brody would march off with Rudy, reaffirming that Brody always considered him more of a brother than Jake. As an only child, that felt good to Rudy.

But this time, for the first time, it didn't happen.

Instead, Brody just looked at Rudy and said, "Sorry, Rudacious, I'll call you later."

"I might not be around later," threatened Rudy, who picked up a snowball in disgust and whipped it at a tree.

"Hey," said Brody. "You almost hit that blue jay."

Rudy didn't respond—with words, that is. He just shot Brody a cold stare. Then, when he realized the blue jay was back on its perch, he picked up another snowball and threw it in the exact same direction.

Part II

The Inspection

Part
3

The Inspection

chapter 18

Punching Crab

The hike to find Felonious Fish was not easy, which was exactly the way Felonious wanted it. Living miles from everyone and everything in his past helped him forget all about spirit animals, Akaways, and the secret portal to Sarraka that had consumed his life for so long. He had a new purpose now, with a job he loved and a home he could afford in a place where no humans of any kind could find him.

Unless, of course, they had that beautiful combination of a map and a mission.

Blazing a new trail with every step, Brody and Jake followed their map, refusing to give up on their mission.

Brody relied heavily on the powers of the Akaway, and Jake consistently called upon the agility and courage of his new spirit animal, the ocelot, and still they barely traversed the frozen waterfall and were nearly trampled by the tower of teetering boulders.

They talked very little, except to say things like, "What's wrong with Rudy?" or "Do you think we're too late?" or "Whoever said 'nothing's impossible' never tried doing the worm on a beanbag chair."

But no matter the obstacle, they continued to persevere, which means they didn't let anything stand in their way—even when it might have been smart to.

"What's up with this?" asked Brody, as he inched his way to the edge of the Cavern of High Winds and peered down into the complete darkness. "The map says there should be a bridge here."

The Cavern of High Winds was difficult to cross using a sturdy wooden bridge with guardrails. The strong gusts of wind were unpredictable. One lapse in concentration and you'd be blown over the edge—no second chances. Imagine how tough it would be when the bridge has been replaced by nothing more than a long and narrow tree trunk, kind of like the one a beaver would use to build a dam.

Jake reached for a large stone and tossed it over the edge. He waited for the sound that never came.

"Must be pretty deep."

"What do you think is down there?" asked Brody.

"Let's not find out," responded Jake.

Then he put his hand out, which basically meant, "After you."

Brody took five deep breaths, all the while concentrating on the balancing powers of a squirrel. He put his first foot on the log and wiggled it around to make sure the footing was secure. It was. Then he put his second foot on and slowly started walking as if he were on a balance beam.

For the first time in his life, Jake took five deep breaths as well.

It couldn't hurt, he thought to himself. And, in fact, it didn't.

Don't look down, he told himself. And, of course, he looked down.

But he took a step and then another and then started

following closely behind Brody, reminding himself to have the same confidence he saw in his little brother. True confidence is a powerful weapon, and soon Brody and Jake were walking across the log as if it were nothing more than a narrow sidewalk next to Grammy's house.

"This doesn't seem so bad," said Brody, accounting for the strong gusts of wind by leaning directly into them.

"Don't get cocky," said Jake, following closely behind. "We still have halfway to go."

"See, that's your problem," said Brody. "You always see the negative. We've made it this far. What could possibly go wrong?"

Before Jake could respond with an insult like, "Your face could go wrong," something went wrong.

It was the log. It started spinning. Slowly at first, then faster and faster. Brody and Jake moved their feet quickly to keep their balance, which actually could have seemed like a pretty fun game—that is, if losing didn't mean falling an unknown distance into the belly of the cavern.

"Very impressive," said a creature with two beady eyes, a reddish brown shell, and two claws, which just happened to be spinning the log. "What are you guys, a couple of lumberjacks?"

For those of you who have never spoken to animals before—I mean, really spoken to animals where they can understand you and you can understand them—it is quite a shock the first time it happens. So it helps to have someone along who shares the same gifts of the Akaway so that when you look at him and say, "Is that crab talking to us?" he can look back and say, "Yes."

Unfortunately, Brody Boondoggle didn't have that. Jake loved his spirit animal. It allowed him to see things kids without a connection to their spirit animals couldn't see, like the cut over Brody's left eye, the blood that still oozed from it, and the very special crab who was spinning the log as if he didn't care if Brody and Jake fell or not. But it didn't help him hear the crab talk.

"You don't hear that crab talking?" Brody asked Jake.

"You do?" answered Jake.

And quickly they both understood that this was just the way it was going to be. They agreed that from this point forward, Brody would translate for Jake every time an animal spoke, and Jake would try his best to accept the fact that Brody could hear animals talking in his head, even if it seemed a little hard to believe.

"You're going to want to keep those feet moving. And keep your heads up and knees bent. It's better for balance," instructed the crab, and Brody heard those words perfectly in his head.

"Thanks for the advice," said Brody, who, true to their agreement, translated the information for Jake.

"Wait a second," said the crab, pointing at Jake. "He can't hear me?"

"Nope," said Brody.

"Can he see me?" asked the crab. He stopped spinning the log for just a second to wave his claws back and forth vigorously the way the boy fiddler crab behaves when he wants to get a girl fiddler crab to like him.

"Yeah, he can see you," said Brody. "But he doesn't want to be your girlfriend."

"Very interesting," said the crab, placing his claws back on the log and turning.

"How about if you just stop spinning this thing," responded Brody, "and I'll explain everything."

"Oh, I don't think that's an option," said the crab. "Too risky. There's obviously something special about you.

Pretty impressive the way you made it through that forest and climbed down the waterfall, especially this time of year. But nobody gets across this cavern. Not while Punching Crab is on the job. So we'll do this my way. You explain everything first. Then, I'll stop spinning the log—if you haven't fallen off already."

"Fair enough," said Brody, trying to sound confident even though it was getting harder and harder to keep his balance on the moving log. "My name is Brody Boondoggle, and this is my brother Jake. We're looking for Felonious Fish. We're on a very important mission."

"Felonious Fish?" said Punching Crab. "He hasn't been called Felonious in a long, long time. Not unless you're a close friend, that is. For everyone else, Felonious goes by the name of Fish Doctor now."

Brody translated that very important piece of information to Jake before responding.

"So you know him?" asked Brody.

"I'm not saying I do and I'm not saying I don't."

"Well, we need to see him," said Brody, as beads of sweat started to form on his face. "It's about the last Akaway."

"Whoa, whoa, whoa," said Punching Crab. "What's an Akaway?"

Brody translated this to Jake, who was breathing harder than Brody was but still gave him the nod to make the joke. "Oh, about 50 pounds."

Punching Crab smiled. But the smile quickly started to fade. "And that's how I know you're a fraud," said Punching Crab. "The last Akaway is dead. I can feel it and so can Felonious. You guys are lying, and if there's one thing I don't like, it's tomatoes, which is strange because I love ketchup. But if there are two things I don't like, it's tomatoes and liars."

"The last Akaway is still alive, but just barely," Brody insisted, with a little attitude, which was probably appropriate for someone who didn't know how much longer he or his brother could last on a spinning log. "That's why we need to open the portal to Sarraka. That's why we need to see Felonious. And that's why you need to stop spinning this 'dam' log."

Brody's passion seemed real to Punching Crab, and the dreamer part of him wanted to believe every word Brody said. But Punching Crab had learned to ignore his dreams lately. After all, they didn't seem to be coming true.

"It doesn't matter if you're lying or if you're not," said Punching Crab, choosing to spin the log even faster. "Felonious can't help you. He doesn't have the power to open the portal. You need the power of the Akaway, and there's not a creature like that anymore. You just have to face it. It's a different world now. There are no more heroes."

As soon as Brody finished translating for Jake, they both looked at each other. Jake glanced up at the cut above Brody's left eye, and then said what they were both thinking.

"Yeah, there are. There's Brody Boondoggle."

Don't Stop
Be-leeding

There was only one way to tell if Brody Boondoggle was truly "the one," and Punching Crab knew it. So without hesitating, he ran right out on the log to inspect the cut over Brody's left eye. The problem was that Punching Crab forgot the log was still spinning, and as soon as his claw hit the log, he went flying.

"Little help?" said Punching Crab meekly, as he dangled from a scrawny branch that seemed to be getting weaker every second.

Brody and Jake looked at each other and rolled their eyes. When the log finally slowed to a complete stop, they took a second to catch their breath, and then they calmly walked to the other side.

"I don't like tomatoes either," said Jake, helping Punching Crab back to safety.

For the first time in his life, Punching Crab was speechless, as rays of hope radiated from his body like sunbeams fighting their way through an overcast sky. Eventually, he conjured up the courage to see if this was for real by crawling up Brody's arm for a better look at the bite just above the outside corner of his left eye.

"I've heard about this, but I never thought it was possible," he said softly, touching the scar with his claw. "And it's still bleeding."

"Yeah," said Brody. "It's been bleeding for more than a week. It won't stop."

"Not until the Akaway is safe," said Punching Crab. "Or until she's dead."

Brody touched his eyebrow, glad to feel the blood on his fingers.

"But this is good news," said Punching Crab, quickly changing the tone back to a celebratory one. "Do you realize what this means?" He didn't wait for an answer. "It means there's hope. After all these years, there's finally hope."

Punching Crab jumped down from Brody's shoulder and impressively started pulling Brody by the backpack to the main trail. "We've gotta get you to Felonious right away."

"Now you're talking my language," said Jake, after Brody translated.

"Well, I should warn you," said Punching Crab. "It's not going to be that easy. He's not a people person like me—or, at least not anymore. Felonious is always on the lookout for unwanted visitors. And he's nearly impossible to catch. He's like a ninja fish. You know what I mean?"

"Not really," said Brody.

"I mean, his days of worrying about the Akaway are over. The memories are too painful. He's moved on."

Punching Crab came to an abrupt stop. Then he motioned for Brody and Jake to come closer, which they did.

"But that was before," he continued. "Everything is different now. Once he knows who you are, that you can open the portal, that there's hope, it'll be different."

"Different?" asked Brody. "Why?"

"Listen to me very carefully," he said. "It's you. You

make all the difference in the world. You make a difference to the kids who have no way to connect to their spirit animals. You make a difference to all the creatures that have dreamed of being part of Sarraka but have never had the chance. And you make a difference to the Akaway, who has given everything to keep hope alive. Don't you see? She bit you for a reason. She didn't have the strength to keep fighting. But you do."

Punching Crab didn't wait for a response. Instead, he continued to lead the way through a variety of hidden passages and trails. But when they finally arrived at the private creek surrounded by the protective forest off an isolated trail where Felonious had lived safely and secretly for years, the fish was gone.

Zebra's Pizza

"Fishnapped," declared Punching Crab in a worried tone that seemed foreign to his personality. Brody and Jake stood still, but their heads moved quickly in all directions, trying to follow their new friend as he scurried around like a gnat in a glass jar, screaming, "It's impossible, it's impossible!"

While Punching Crab tried to determine what was possible and what wasn't, Jake began walking around the creek, picking up branches, checking under rocks, and reviewing the notes from his research.

"What are you doing?" asked Brody, jogging to catch up.

"I just can't believe it would be so easy to capture that fish," said Jake. "He just seems too smart. And didn't Punching Crab call him a ninja fish?"

"Well maybe he's not as ninja as he thinks," said Brody.

"Maybe," said Jake. "But look at this."

He identified two fresh sets of footprints surrounding the creek. "One with four legs. One with two," Jake surmised, which means he figured it out based on the pattern of the prints. "We didn't see footprints throughout this entire hike. Now all of a sudden we see these. Do you think that's an accident?"

Looking for clues seemed kind of fun, so Brody thought of a bloodhound, and he started sniffing around as well. "And check this out," he said shortly afterward. Brody motioned to the wool hat Felonious had been wearing in all of his pictures. It was dangling from a branch just above them.

"He's gone, all right," confirmed Jake. "But something's not as it seems."

They walked back to Punching Crab, who was taking five deep breaths that were surprisingly similar to the ones Grammy took when she first saw the Akaway.

"You feeling better?" asked Brody.

"Better," acknowledged Punching Crab.

"Good. Now we have to figure this out. You must have seen something," said Brody, as if he were a detective interviewing a prime witness. "Did anyone come here before us?"

"No," said Punching Crab.

"Nobody?" questioned Jake.

"Nobody," repeated Punching Crab firmly. "Nobody at all. I'm telling you, it was just you, the pizza delivery guy, and his zebra. That's it."

Brody dropped his head.

"What?" Jake asked, waiting for a translation.

"You don't want to know," said Brody.

"Pizza delivery guy?" Jake yelled, when Brody finally translated.

"Yeah," said Punching Crab. "He showed up a few hours before you guys."

"Well, did you spin the log?" asked Brody sternly. "What happened to, 'Nobody gets across this cavern, not while Punching Crab is on the job'?"

"Why would I spin the log?" asked Punching Crab

innocently. "The zebra might have fallen. It was a funny-looking zebra, but that doesn't mean I wanted it to fall."

Brody gritted his teeth as he asked the next question, slowly enunciating each word. "Don't you think it was strange that a guy was delivering a pizza—WITH A ZEBRA?"

"Not really," said Punching Crab. "The pizza was from Zebra's Pizza. It said so right on the box. The guy couldn't have been nicer. I tipped him 20 clams."

Now it was Jake's turn to grit his teeth.

"One more question," he said. "When was the last time Felonious ordered a pizza?"

"Oh, never, he hates pizza. He has an incredible loyalty to anchovies," said Punching Crab, and that's when the reality finally hit him. "Wait a second, you don't think that guy was an imposter, do you?"

Brody and Jake paused appropriately and then said in unison, "It's possible."

Punching Crab said nothing more. Instead he quietly walked over to a hole in the creek, plugged his nose with one of his claws, and jumped.

Paranoid

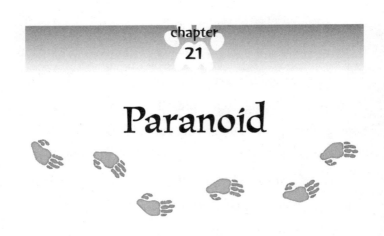

Seconds passed, then minutes, and it soon became obvious that there was no way to know what Punching Crab was doing, how long he would be gone, or if he would even come back.

"How long do you think he'll be down there?" asked Brody, periodically poking his head in and out of the holes in the ice.

"I don't know," said Jake, who was passing the time by tossing rocks at a tree stump on the other side of the creek.

"Do you think we were too hard on him?" asked Brody.

"I'm not sure how hard you're supposed to be on a crab who fell for the old Zebra's Pizza trick," said Jake. "I guess all we can do now is wait."

Brody shrugged, picked up a handful of rocks, and started throwing them at the tree stump as well. Before they knew it, they were involved in a pretty intense game of "hit the stump with the rock."

"Who's winning?" said Punching Crab, as he pulled himself out of the creek with his front claws while holding a strange looking frog with his back claws. He didn't wait for an answer. Secure on the land, Punching Crab shifted the frog and started twisting the head around and around until it finally popped right off.

"Don't worry," said Punching Crab. "It's not real. Frogs are our friends."

It was actually one of those fake frogs that make great hiding places for house keys—only a little bigger. Inside was no house key but an electronic device that Jake recognized immediately. Punching Crab then explained— and Brody translated—what the word *paranoid* means, which is basically when you think there's always someone trying to get you. Apparently, Felonious Fish was paranoid, so he placed a tracking device in his fin.

"Like the ones some people put in their dogs,"

described Punching Crab. "This will lead us right to him."

"You think we should go after him?" asked Brody.

"Isn't that why you came here?" replied Punching Crab.

Brody and Jake shrugged as if to say, "good point," as Punching Crab started furiously hitting and twisting and flipping the tracking device. Finally, Jake grabbed the remote from Punching Crab and, in a single motion, flipped it on. Within seconds, Jake maneuvered through the appropriate settings, and they were on their way to yet another adventure.

Felonious had done a masterly job on the transmitter. It was sort of like a video game, and the sophisticated graphics led Jake, Brody, and Punching Crab through another challenging hike deep into the forest.

They didn't talk much, except to say things like, "We're halfway there," or "Are you getting hungry?" or "Would you rather swim in a pool filled with dog drool or press your tongue into your principal's nostril?"

But it had been several hours since breakfast, and the lack of food was leading to a lack of energy, which led to two grumpy brothers. And everyone knows when brothers get grumpy, they lose their patience, and then they start to blame each other for things like bumping into a prickly bush or slipping down a steep decline or just breathing.

"What's wrong with you?" yelled Jake.

"I didn't do anything," replied Brody. "What's wrong with you?"

"Your face is wrong with me."

As the two brothers inched closer together, Punching Crab jumped in the middle.

"Maybe we should take a break and have a nice peaceful lunch," suggested Punching Crab. And given a few seconds to consider the option, Jake and Brody begrudgingly agreed—except for the peaceful part.

"Do you have to chew like that?" yelled Brody, as Jake gobbled down cheese and crackers.

"I'm allowed to eat my lunch," barked Jake, who instantly started chomping a little louder. "Just ignore it."

"I can't ignore it," said Brody. "You sound like a pig scarfing bubble gum."

"Maybe it's some animal out there sending chomping noises directly into your brain," suggested Jake.

"At least I've got a brain," responded Brody. "You've got more rocks in your head than you do in your pocket."

"Do you guys do this often?" asked Punching Crab, amused by the fact that they could go from a fun hike to a fight in such a short amount of time.

"We're brothers," explained Brody, who didn't bother translating for Jake.

It was relatively silent after that, as each brother consumed a banana, a handful of chocolate cat cookies, and a peanut-butter granola bar.

Jake tried sending Brody a few harsh thoughts through the air, but based on Brody's lack of reaction, he was pretty sure it didn't work, which actually bummed him out.

Jake imagined how cool it would be to communicate with animals telepathically without having to speak. It made him realize that he secretly admired Brody for believing that it could really be possible. And the funny thing was, when Jake's aura became a little less angry, Brody seemed a little better too. He handed Jake "ants on a log" (celery with peanut butter and raisins) as a peace offering. Jake accepted and even chewed it quietly—kind of.

"See, that's much better," said Punching Crab. "Felonious never understood that old saying that we always hurt the ones we love. He always thought that it's the ones we love that we should treat the best."

Brody rolled his eyes. Jake did the same after Brody translated.

"So if Felonious is so smart," said Brody, "why'd he leave the spirit animal world? Why'd he give up on Sarraka?"

"That's a long story," said Punching Crab.

"Well, we have a long hike ahead of us," said Brody.

"Truché," responded Punching Crab, which was his own made-up way of saying, "Good point."

So, with their stomachs full and their curiosity peaked, Brody and Jake were back on the trail, moving steadily while completely focused on Punching Crab's every word.

"Let's see," said Punching Crab, who was hitching a ride on Brody's backpack. "What's the best way to explain this? Okay. I guess it's best to start at the beginning."

Punching Crab waited for Brody to translate for Jake—he was getting used to that by now. Then his tone turned more serious.

"I want you to picture a time when Sarraka and the rest of the universe were as one," Punching Crab began. "It was perfect harmony. Kids were automatically connected to their spirit animals, which gave them their special powers and filled the world with plenty of positive energy. Children, Akaways, and all the other magical creatures flourished. There was balance in the universe, and everything was good."

"I can picture that," said Brody.

"Yeah," said Punching Crab, who seemed to be picturing it as well. "It was a pretty special time."

"So what happened?" asked Brody.

"Something came along and things started to change," described Punching Crab.

"What?"

"It's hard to say exactly," said Punching Crab. "It could have been so many things. Distractions really. Complicated distractions that most kids couldn't resist. Over time, fewer and fewer kids were connected to their spirit animals, and things got out of balance. Something had to be done. So, at that point, spirit animal energy was borrowed from Sarraka, kind of like a loan. It seemed harmless enough until we had to start borrowing more and more. Eventually, Sarraka started to suffer as well. It was getting weaker.

Easier to attack."

"But who would want to attack Sarraka?"

"Only anyone who was interested in unlimited power," said Punching Crab. "The attacks kept coming, and it was only a matter of time before they would get in."

"Before who would get in?"

"That's the mystery," said Punching Crab. "No one knew. So, to protect Sarraka, it was closed off. The only way to get there now is through a portal. With Sarraka safe, the Akaways bravely stayed behind in this world, to keep the connections going. The Akaways wanted to save the children."

"Save them how?" asked Brody.

"By giving them a chance," said Punching Crab. "The kids who proved they were strong enough to fight the distractions would be connected to their spirit animals by the Akaways. The plan was that when enough kids were connected to bring balance back to the universe, the Akaways would open the portal and return home safely. Unfortunately, that never happened. In fact, it was just the opposite, and with the spirit animal energy fading in our world, the Akaways started to suffer as well. At first, we saw it in little ways—their senses dulled, they couldn't see as clearly or hear as well. Then it got more serious, and then it was too late. They didn't have the strength to open the portal and go home."

"So that's why Felonious wanted to do it," interjected Jake, who was reviewing his research as Punching Crab spoke. "It would give the Akaways the energy they needed to survive and allow kids the chance to connect themselves to their own spirit animals."

"Exactly," said Punching Crab. "Felonious knew the power of Sarraka. He used to say that its energy could make all your dreams come true. He tried to convince everyone that the portal needed to be reopened. But they wouldn't allow it."

"Why not?" asked Jake.

"The general consensus was that kids couldn't handle it," said Punching Crab. "Couldn't handle the responsibility. But again, Felonious fought back. He argued that children were capable of much more than anyone gave them credit for. He put his reputation on the line. 'They can do it,' he promised. 'They won't let us down.'"

"So what happened?" asked Brody.

"They let us down," said Punching Crab. "Felonious was devastated. That's when he quit. He continued to try to open the portal on his own. He became obsessed even, like his life depended on it. But he couldn't do it. And when all the Akaways started dying, finally Felonious had had enough. That's when he became a doctor, and he hasn't thought about the last Akaway since."

There's nothing better than a compelling story to make a tough hike go faster, and when Punching Crab was done, there wasn't time for follow-up questions, although Brody and Jake had plenty. The transmitter had done its job, revealing the exact location of Felonious Fish, which meant it was now time to stop learning about his past and to start worrying about his future.

Nasty Perfume

The three-story house stood on the top of a massive hill, with just the right amount of snow to make it perfect for sledding. The bricks on the house had been painted white, but that must have been a long time ago because the color was faded on most of them. The black shutters around all the windows and the balcony surrounding the second level appeared more ominous, as if trying to warn intruders to enter at their own risk.

So that's exactly what Jake, Brody, and Punching Crab did.

Working together, they quickly built a pretty sweet snow ramp and easily cruised right over the imposing wooden fence that surrounded the house. Once safely on the other side, they created an identical ramp just in case they needed a speedy escape.

"We'll meet here if we get split up," instructed Brody.

Perfect sledding hills are great to slide down, but they can really burn the leg muscles on the way up. Climbing steadily for what seemed like forever, Brody, Jake, and Punching Crab finally reached the top of the hill, and, after circling the house, felt rewarded to find an open door around the back. They tracked a small sliver of light through what they assumed was the basement of the house until they reached another door that led to the main level. Jake turned the knob slowly to the left, and there was a faint "pop." The door creaked open, and, like three little mice, everyone scurried in.

"This thing doesn't get any more specific," said Jake, referring to the transmitter. "We're going to have to find him the old-fashioned way now."

"No problem," said Brody, "You guys search upstairs. I'll look around down here. If you see anything, be like an ash-throated crake and caw, caw, caw." He practiced the birdcall in a soft and lyrical voice. "That will be the warning sign."

"Caw, caw," Punching Crab and Jake practiced before they quickly and quietly crept up the stairs, stepping on the outside of each step so there wouldn't be a creak. Once they reached the top, Jake and Punching Crab walked in opposite directions down a hallway that was as long and narrow as a bowling alley. After several slow, soft steps, they each arrived at a door.

Jake was first to reach for the knob on the door in front of him. That's when he noticed an ominous green light coming from a door a little farther down the hall. It was like an eerie energy oozing out of the bottom of the door, and Jake's little voice told him to check that room next.

For now, he turned back to the door in front of him. He took one last deep breath, and then he went in. One step later, he heard a sound.

Click.

It was the same noise he had heard when chasing the dogcatcher and Doodad, and Jake worried that he would be flung feet first right through the ceiling. But that didn't happen. This time, when he tripped on a wire, he was sprayed with a subtle mist of what seemed like perfume—

nasty perfume. It smelled more like raw meat. Disoriented at first, Jake staggered back to the door that led to the hallway, but it was already locked behind him. He pulled and kicked, but the door wouldn't budge. Jake had seen movies where big, tough guys kicked down doors, and he decided this would be a good time to give it a try. But as he backed up for a running start, he tripped a second wire that stretched across the middle of the room.

Click.

A small trapdoor in the corner of the room swung open. Jake's eyes bulged, and his jaw dropped, as he now understood why the perfume smelled like meat. Because that's what puppies love. And right now, Jake counted about 13 of them heading straight for him.

chapter 23

Reunited

The puppies could have been training for the World Barking Championship, and Punching Crab still wouldn't have heard them. His full attention was focused on his best friend, who was lying in the middle of the very first room he entered.

"Stay back, old friend," warned Felonious, but Punching Crab didn't listen. Maybe if he had, he would have recognized that this was no ordinary room.

"Are you okay?" yelled Punching Crab, recklessly sprinting to the aid of his buddy. "Are you hurt? Let's get you out of here."

But that wasn't going to happen. Because Punching

Crab's left claw had just activated a kind of crab trap he had never seen before.

His beady eyes looked straight down to what appeared to be a large platform in the shape of a snowboard emerging from directly underneath, and it was currently lifting both Felonious and Punching Crab slowly into the air.

The bigger problem was that, by the time Punching Crab realized what was happening, it was too late to jump. And that was probably a good thing, because if he had jumped, it would have been right into a giant, steaming, fully functioning hot tub that now had them completely surrounded.

chapter
24

Baby Joey

The problem wasn't that Brody Boondoggle didn't feel the vibrations from the hot tub bursting out of the floor or hear the 13 puppies pouncing on a human Milk Bone just one level above. The problem was, at the moment, he was too distracted to care.

That's what happens when you go exploring for clues, and the very first room you see seems to be calling your name: *Brody Boondoggle*. It was that voice, but not really. *Come in and play.*

And how could he not? Right in the middle of the room was an oversized, bright red, fluffy, beanbag chair, with a cup of steaming hot chocolate with extra whipped cream that seemed to be waiting just for him. A rectangular table acted as a bridge between the chair and a big-screen, high-definition television set with surround sound. On the table were a remote control, a video game controller, and a helmet, complete with tinted visor and microphone.

Normally, this temptation would be no match for a child whose spirit animal was an Akaway. But Brody was up against a powerful foe, and one of the foe's powers was knowing exactly how to pique the curiosity of an 11-year-old boy.

Brody stayed low to the ground as he crept his way inside the room that was calling his name.

Come closer, closer, the voice seemed to whisper, and Brody couldn't resist.

He melted into the chair and, instantly, felt as warm and treasured as a baby joey in his mother's pouch.

"Caw, caw, caw."

It was the warning call. Something must not be right.

"Caw, caw, caw."

He heard it again, but Brody didn't listen.

"Caw, caw," the final "caw" faded into the distance, which was just fine with Brody, because things seemed just fine to him. And the only voice he was listening to now was the one that told him to turn on the video game, aim the arrow at the big red target, and push down with his right thumb to begin.

Tackle

Even as Jake ducked and dodged to protect himself from all the different breeds of puppies, a small part of him had a little appreciation for whoever created this trap—because although Alaskan malamutes and Yorkshire terriers; Great Danes and miniature poodles; assorted mutts and the purest of purebreds can relentlessly nip, scratch, claw, and tug, especially when they see what seems like a big meat-smelling bone just waiting for them in the middle of an empty room, they were also so incredibly adorable that it was pretty hard to fight them off.

"Sit," Jake ordered. Nobody sat.

"Stay," Jake commanded. But that didn't work. Neither

did "heel," "roll over," "shake," "down," or "release."

In almost no time, Jake's coat was ripped, his neck was scratched, and he was missing a mitten. After a few seconds of running, his ankles were attacked, his back was scratched, and he was finally brought down by what looked like a beagle-shepherd mix, a puppy Jake named Tackle.

The only advantage to lying on the ground in a fetal position with his arms covering his face as Tackle and his buddies relentlessly harassed him was that Jake was so tired that he felt like he could easily fall asleep by simply closing his eyes.

And that's when he heard the voice.

Play with them.

Jake looked around and saw nothing with fewer than four legs. Maybe he did fall asleep, and it was a dream. Maybe it was Brody, a connection through their spirit animals, but Jake didn't believe that for more than a moment. Regardless of where it came from, when Jake considered the idea, it actually sounded pretty ingenious.

"Puppies play hard and they sleep hard," he remembered, and he realized that right now, they weren't playing nearly hard enough.

Play with them.

And this time, he decided to listen.

It's amazing how a great idea can give you just the burst of adrenaline you need to pop from the ground seconds after you think you might have just fallen asleep. Upright and alert, Jake quickly yanked off his hat, tucked it into a ball, and threw it against the wall. A black Labrador retriever, a silver and gray collie, and a little Dalmatian that Jake naturally called Spot sprinted after the hat, with Spot getting there first and playing a little keep-away with the other two dogs Jake had named Fetch and Chase.

Jake didn't stop to appreciate how well the dogs played together; he was too busy unwrapping his scarf. He offered one end to a labradoodle, whom Jake named Vise because of the hold she had on the end of the scarf. Vise pulled. Jake pulled back. Vise pulled a little harder. Jake pulled even harder still. As if trying to show Jake how it was done, an Old English sheepdog took over, and, before you knew it, Vise and Grip were yanking and pulling each other all around the room.

By now, Spot, Fetch, and Chase were back, and Jake grabbed the slobbery hat from Spot's mouth and was about to throw it again. But then he paused.

"Sit," he said, as if he really believed they might listen. And they did. All of them. "Good dogs," he said and tossed his hat. This time Chase got it, which was appropriate, because now he was playing keep-away, and the other dogs were hot on his trail.

This gave Jake a chance to use his remaining mitten as a sponge to rub some of the beef-smelling perfume off his arms and legs. He then held the mitten to the noses of two more dogs, and when it seemed like Seek and Hide were just about ready to burst, Jake slid the mitten into the sleeve of his jacket and flung it through the trapdoor.

"Find the mitten," and that's exactly what Seek and Hide tried to do.

Half an hour goes pretty quickly when you're being challenged both mentally and physically, and for all that time, Jake felt like a juggler at the circus trying to keep as many balls and scarves and mittens as possible in the air at once. He even pulled off his boots, ripped off his heavy wool socks, rolled them into balls, and started throwing them as well.

It wasn't until after he had a spare moment to enjoy the

carefree play of Seek, Hide, Spot, Chase, Fetch, Vise, Grip, and the five other dogs he hadn't had a chance to name that he realized something was missing.

"Where's Tackle?" he thought, scanning the room. "Tackle!" he yelled. "Tackle!"

There weren't too many places to go in this room, so it didn't take long to find Tackle in the closet, completely passed out on Jake's jacket.

Something about just gazing at a sleeping puppy makes you feel good, and Jake allowed himself a little extra time to feel this way before whispering, "That's a good puppy." When he turned around to face the room, the feeling multiplied as he whispered the same thing a dozen more times. All the puppies were cuddled up and asleep. Completely exhausted.

Mission One complete, he thought. Now it's time to escape.

He pointed two fingers to his eyes, then the door, and said, "You're going down."

He ran full speed, lowering his shoulder like Walter Payton, who was one of the toughest running backs of all time.

Thud.

Unfortunately, Jake wasn't one of the toughest running backs of all time yet, so the door didn't properly respect his charge. Jake crumbled to the ground, grabbing his right shoulder. Big, salty tears filled up his eyes and rolled down his cheeks. But they didn't last long because there was a big, wet, slobbery tongue to wipe them away.

"Tackle." Jake smiled when he saw the little mutt by his side. Tackle wagged his tail and licked away as if to say, "Everything will be all right."

Or maybe he was saying, "You better get going, because if I'm awake, the rest of the puppies might not be sleeping for as long as you think." Jake tilted his head and, for just a second, allowed himself to believe that he understood.

"But how am I going to get out of here?" he asked. Of course, Tackle couldn't answer. He was just a puppy. But he did twist his head toward the wall where a window should be.

"There are no windows," Jake said, but Tackle kept staring at that one spot on the wall. And that's when Jake realized that maybe he could speak with animals after all. Oh, he couldn't understand them literally without Brody there to translate. But he liked Tackle. He had spirit and spunk, and when Jake looked into those deep brown eyes, he might not have been able to understand what Tackle said word for word, but he was pretty sure he could figure out what he meant.

I saw windows from the outside, he thought. *They must be covered up from the inside.*

With his right arm held tightly across his chest, Jake ran his left fingers against the wooden panel on the wall. It didn't take long to find the seam. Wedging his fingers in, he pulled back to reveal a window.

"Good dog." And Tackle wagged his tail in a way that seemed to imply, "Happy to help."

The strength in Jake's left arm alone caused the window to nearly fly through the top of the ceiling as he opened it. After inspecting his mittens and socks, Jake decided to leave those behind, but he quickly slid on his boots, hat, and jacket. He put one leg through the open window and ducked his head down and through, with his other leg following closely behind.

Standing on the balcony, Jake hoped he would see Brody and Punching Crab safely outside by the getaway ramp, but he wasn't at all surprised when he didn't. But he did see something else: It was a shed.

Tools, he thought to himself. *That's just what I need.*

Jake looked down and estimated that the distance to the ground was about the same as the high dive at the public pool, but now there was no water waiting below. And it's not like Jake was an expert diver. He still remembered the belly flop that left his stomach bright red for a couple hours. He couldn't even imagine what would happen if he landed on his right shoulder, even with the cushion of the snow.

Jake scanned the area quickly for another way, but there was none. He prepared himself mentally with five deep breaths.

Don't look down, he told himself. But, of course, he looked down. Then he jumped.

His mind was clear, almost peaceful, as he naturally twisted in the air. Had someone been watching—which they were—it must have appeared magical, but to Jake, it seemed natural when he landed perfectly balanced on his feet, as easily as if he were jumping from the top bunk of his bed. As if he were an ocelot.

Uncle
Skeeta

The virtual graphics that seemed to hover in the air slightly above his helmet painted an inauspicious picture for Brody Boondoggle, which meant that he was losing the game he was now obsessed with. But still, he would never stop trying.

What Brody didn't know was that he couldn't stop even if he wanted to. The man in the next room monitoring the whole house with a high-capacity surveillance system wouldn't allow it. At least not until the one very important gauge on the game—the one Brody never noticed, the one that measured his spirit animal level—fell just a little bit further. It would happen any minute now, and the man allowed a modest grin to appear because he knew there was nothing Brody could do to stop it.

Brody's wrists and ankles were strapped to the chair, but they were only physical restraints. His mind was also locked in, lost in a world that had been created just for that purpose.

Then suddenly, the grin on the man's face started to fade as he watched Jake escape from the room on the second floor. He saw him leap from the balcony with an obviously wounded shoulder and dart into the shed. And he was now well aware of the fact that Jake was currently approaching the solid mahogany wood doors that guarded the only way in or out of the game room on a high-performance, heavy-duty riding lawn mower called the Rhino2000.

Maybe these kids aren't hopeless after all, the man thought to himself.

There was no hope for those doors. As advertised, the Rhino2000 burst through anything in its way, and, in this case, the mahogany doors were shredded like mozzarella cheese. Jake and the Rhino2000 pulled right up to Brody.

"Get on!" Jake ordered.

But Brody didn't respond. He couldn't. He was trapped, a bright yellow cocoon surrounding his body. Jake remembered that cocoon. Then he saw the spirit-animal-level gauge on the screen and knew instantly what was happening. Jake focused on the bite on the outside corner of Brody's left eye. It was almost dry. What little spirit-animal energy Brody had left was being drained.

Jake grabbed the remote and clicked. Nothing. He drove a few feet forward and pushed the power button on the television. Still nothing. Quickly, he scanned the room for an outlet. The power had to be coming from somewhere.

"It's wireless."

The man standing by the opening created by the lawn mower was almost singing the words, with his arms outstretched as if he were revealing the secret to a magic trick.

"The power comes from a room upstairs," the man continued. "Go ahead and check it out if you want. Oh, I forgot, you were already up there. Decided not to investigate that room? Don't feel bad. You couldn't have gotten in even if you tried."

This man was familiar. He wasn't particularly big

or noticeably small. His shaved head and dark bushy eyebrows only highlighted his ocean-blue eyes. Jake recognized the eyes.

"So, how's that shoulder of yours?" the man asked, in a soft, genuine tone.

"It hurts," Jake said honestly.

"I'll bet. These doors are solid. Takes more than a shoulder to knock them down," said the man. He then acknowledged the broken door beneath his feet. "But you already figured that out. You did a great job with those puppies too."

Jake tried to fight the instinct to respond but couldn't.

"Thanks."

"You must be thirsty," the man continued. "Can I offer you something to drink? How about something to eat?"

This guy was good. Not only was he mercilessly draining Brody's spirit-animal energy, but he was also a gracious host at the same time. Jake peered over at Brody, who was obviously still lost in the video game. He considered making a break to save him, but without Brody's help and with only one arm, he wouldn't be strong enough to pull him away.

Brody, Jake thought to himself, trying to send Brody a signal that would break him out of his trance, but Brody didn't move. Finally, he just yelled, "Brody! Brody!" But still no connection.

"Don't worry about him," continued the man, as if nothing bad was happening. "Come on now." He waved his arms around the room at all the different bowls of fruit and candy. There was even a fountain that provided 13 different types of soda. "Help yourself to anything you want. Then you can join your brother. You know you want to play."

Jake was both hungry and thirsty, but that's not why he finally made the decision to eat. He looked around at all his favorite foods, and then he saw the one bowl he couldn't resist, and he knew he had to have it.

"An excellent choice," said the man, after Jake drove the Rhino2000 only a few feet to the treat. "It's the world's best gourmet taffy. And I have a dozen different kinds: chocolate malt, cream soda, key lime pie, banana split, candy corn, and caramel swirl. Try any one you like."

Jake unwrapped the first piece of gourmet taffy he touched and threw it in his mouth. It was tropical punch, and it was good. The man simply watched as Jake grabbed another piece and then another. Filling his mouth with coconut, chocolate chip, and maple syrup, his jaws were in constant motion. Chewing over and over, louder and louder—like a pig scarfing bubble gum.

Bad for Business

It was the one sound Brody couldn't ignore. His eyes blinked. The man didn't notice—he had his back to Brody —but Jake did. He noticed because it was the first time Brody blinked since he'd been there.

He's free, Jake thought to himself, as the yellow glow surrounding Brody started to fade. Free from the trance, that is. Now he just needed to break free from the game. Jake knew Brody could do it, now that he had a jolt to get him started. He just needed time. So that's just what Jake gave him. Jake turned his attention back to the man in front of him and started asking questions, both out of curiosity and also to keep the man's attention away from Brody.

"Who are you, and what do you want?" Jake asked confidently.

The splinters from the door creaked beneath his feet as the man reached for a chair and sat down. "Who am I? You can call me Uncle Skeeta," he said. "And what do I want? Let's see." Uncle Skeeta thought briefly before answering, "A law against bedtimes. Five-day weekends. Someone to create a delicious kind of ice cream that is as good for you as baby spinach."

"That would be good," mumbled Jake.

"But I'm not holding my breath for any of those things," said Uncle Skeeta. "So I've taken matters into my own hands. I make video games."

"You make what?" asked Jake, as if it were the last thing he expected to hear.

"That's right," Uncle Skeeta said proudly. "All those amazing video games like the one your brother here is playing right now. Pretty impressive, huh?"

Jake nodded before asking, "So what does that have to do with fishnapping?"

"Hey there, little man," said Uncle Skeeta defensively. "Let's not be throwing around serious accusations that we can't prove. Felonious is just fine. He's upstairs with your crab friend right now."

Jake thought for just a second before continuing. "Well, what do you want with him?" he asked. "With Felonious, that is."

"Oh, you disappoint me," said Uncle Skeeta. "You don't even know what you stumbled into, do you? Well, let me tell you: The video game business is limitless. Pretty much unstoppable. Pretty much, that is. The only thing that could stop us is. . . ." He paused for effect, then without looking, stuck out a finger and pointed it directly at Brody. "Him."

"Brody?" asked Jake. "How can he stop you? And why do you even need to be stopped? Everyone loves video games."

"You would think so," said Uncle Skeeta. "But let me ask you this: Since you've been connected with your spirit animal, how many video games have you played?"

Jake felt the one he carried in his back pocket. He was starting to forget it was even there.

"I still play with it," Jake said. "Just not as much."

"Well, that's just not good enough," said Uncle Skeeta.

"Don't you see, these spirit animals are bad for business."
Uncle Skeeta shook his head slowly. "You gotta see the big
picture. This is about more than video games, it's about
making dreams come true."

Jake looked deep into Uncle Skeeta's eyes, and, at that
point, it didn't take long to figure out whose dreams he
was talking about and just how far he was willing to go to
make them come true.

"So it was you?" Jake said, remembering the encounter
at the lake. "You were that hunter." Jake anxiously looked
around for Gizmo, who was nowhere to be found. "And
you were the dogcatcher too. And the pizza man. Zebra's
pizza? Come on. You're not fooling anyone with those
disguises," Jake claimed.

"Fool you?" responded Uncle Skeeta. "I wasn't trying to
fool anybody. . . ." Uncle Skeeta corrected himself. "Well,
I was trying to fool that little crab, but that was so easy I
almost felt bad."

"So why'd you dress up like that?"

Something changed in Uncle Skeeta's face, and Jake
could sense the disappointment in his eyes. "You really
need to ask a question like that?" said Uncle Skeeta. "I do

it because it's fun. And you should know that. You're not the only one with a spirit animal. I'm a chameleon."

Jake felt foolish, angry, and kind of impressed all at the same time. He didn't need an adult to tell him about fun. But Uncle Skeeta was clearly no ordinary adult. And he clearly knew how to have fun.

"But you followed us home. You stole the map."

"Had to," said Uncle Skeeta. "It gave me a great chance to get to know my enemies. And there's no better way to know people than to infiltrate their surroundings."

Jake stared blankly, and Uncle Skeeta knew why. He rolled his eyes.

"Infiltrate their surroundings?" Jake repeated.

"See where they live. See what they like to do. You can't take that stuff personally. It's just business," explained Uncle Skeeta.

"So tell me," Jake continued. "Was it also fun to shoot the Akaway, or was that business too?"

"Hey, hey, hey," said Uncle Skeeta, who appeared genuinely offended. "You need to know that I love Akaways. I love all animals as much as your brother does. And that's the truth. But I had no other choice. I have a plan, and I can't let anything or any animal stand in my way."

Uncle Skeeta ignored the look from Jake that basically meant he did have other choices beyond hurting the last Akaway. "The only problem was the Akaway was too smart," Uncle Skeeta continued. "It knew it was getting weaker. It knew it didn't have much time. So it transferred its power to your brother. That's what happened at the lake. Not many kids around that are capable of holding so much power. But your brother is one of them." Uncle Skeeta shook his head sadly. "Or he was one of them."

Jake took a deep breath, trying to process everything he had just heard. He didn't know what to do next. But he had done enough. He had given Brody enough time to finally break free from the game.

"You'll never get away with this." That came from Brody, the yellow cocoon now completely gone. He tried to appear confident, but that's hard to do when your spirit has been sucked almost completely away.

When Uncle Skeeta shook his head and clicked his tongue, it was the first time he actually seemed like an adult. "Oh, little man, maybe you do have a little spirit left in you," he said. "But I didn't get this far in life by making mistakes."

He glanced at the spirit-animal-level gauge, which now read *Dangerously Low*. "Your power is practically gone," Uncle Skeeta said. "You're nowhere near strong enough to open the portal. And if you don't, we both know what's going to happen to the last Akaway. Don't you see? It's over. And I only tell you this now because there's absolutely nothing you or your brother can do about it."

Like most kids, Brody Boondoggle and his big brother Jake have a long history of selective hearing, which basically means they hear what they want to hear and ignore the rest. So it shouldn't be too surprising that when Uncle Skeeta told them that there was absolutely nothing they could do about the spirit animal situation, Jake and Brody chose not to listen to that either.

"It's not over until the fat elephant sings," said Brody in his toughest, most forceful voice. He then shrugged innocently when Uncle Skeeta looked at him as if to say, "Is that the best line you got?"

Sadly, it was. Still weak and weary, Brody called on every last bit of spirit in his body to rip off his helmet, pull off the restraints from his arms and legs, and bounce from the chair. He sprinted to Jake, and in one fluid motion, reached below the Rhino2000 and pulled out a long green Weedwacker.

"Don't take another step," he threatened. But Uncle Skeeta just smiled.

"Easy does it," replied Uncle Skeeta with his hands in the air. "I don't believe in fighting. Violence only begets more violence. Make love, not war. Why can't we all just get along?"

"We'll get along fine, once the Akaway is safe," yelled Brody, who then took his position behind Jake on the back of the Rhino2000.

Uncle Skeeta didn't even try to stop them. Mostly, because he had no interest in battling two angry kids and a loaded Weedwacker. As he watched Jake and Brody slowly puttering away like a land snail running from a ground beetle, a menacing smile formed on his face because everything was going just the way he planned.

Wings and a Stiff Breeze

Had Punching Crab known help was awkwardly plowing its way up the stairs on a Rhino2000, he probably wouldn't have attempted such a daring escape on his own. But the truth was that Punching Crab had been looking for an opportunity to be a real hero since he was a young crab, spending his time alone with his dreams of being a spirit animal instead of avoiding crab traps and pinching the butts of little children on the beach like the rest of the crabs his age.

"I think I can make it," said Punching Crab, calculating the distance from the end of the platform to the edge of the hot tub. He had just finished telling Felonious all about

Brody Boondoggle and was too inspired to do nothing.

"No, you can't," said Felonious.

Punching Crab recalculated the distances.

"Yup, I can do this."

Felonious could only watch as Punching Crab paced to the edge of the platform, reached down, and scratched a big X in the wood. Then, with his eyes fixed on the target, he backed away step by step.

"Please," Felonious said in a tone that seemed to contain genuine concern. "You don't have to do this. Everything is going to be fine. Really."

But Punching Crab did have to do this, and Felonious knew it. So he stepped out of the way and, for the first time in a long time, hoped he was wrong.

As Punching Crab limbered up for his big jump, Jake and Brody had already made it up the stairs and were on their way to help. They just needed to make one little detour.

"We're busting in there," said Jake, as he and Brody stood face-to-face with the door to the room Uncle Skeeta dared them to go in. The one right down the hall from Punching Crab. The one with the green glow.

Jake backed up the Rhino2000 and banged straight into those mahogany doors. Unfortunately, the only thing dented was the Rhino2000. Once again, Uncle Skeeta was right. Nothing was breaking down that door. Not even the Rhino2000, no matter how many times Jake backed it up and rammed it in.

"Go ahead and keep trying. You'll never get in there," said Uncle Skeeta. His voice was coming through an intercom by the side of the door. "This is the most secure door ever invented. It's locked with a series of beams made from an indestructible metal alloy. And there is no key."

"So how do you get in, straws?" guessed Jake, noticing a cupful hanging next to the intercom.

"Close," said Uncle Skeeta. "Spit. More specifically, my spit. And only my spit. The computer that operates the door will unlock it only when it recognizes my saliva. What do you think about that?"

Honestly, Jake and Brody thought it was pretty sweet, and they wanted one for their house. But they chose not to answer. Instead, Jake snatched a straw, collected a big wad of his own spit, and shot it into the target by the side of the door.

"Analyzing saliva," came a computerized voice from the speaker. Seconds later, blaring alarms rang throughout the hall as the same voice reported, "Access denied," and then repeated, "Stranger on the premises. Alert Uncle Skeeta. He's the greatest."

Uncle Skeeta finally shut off the alarm, just in time for Punching Crab to hear the final warning from Felonious Fish.

"Come on, now," Felonious pleaded. "You can't be serious."

But Punching Crab had never been more serious. This was his moment, and in just a few steps, he was power crab-walking faster than he had ever walked before. Driving his legs harder and harder, he reached the X, and when he did, Punching Crab did not hesitate. In a smooth, swift motion, he launched himself into the air as if his life depended on it, which it did.

For a second, Punching Crab knew what it was like to fly. Unfortunately, he needed to know that feeling for about two more seconds because the next sound in the room was the echo of a loud, deep kerplunk.

Cotton Balls

Sitting at the bottom of the hot tub, Punching Crab wasn't waiting for Felonious to dive in after him. He knew Felonious wasn't that kind of cat, and Punching Crab's one regret wasn't his decision to try to escape. Given the situation again, he'd make the same choice. No, his only regret was. . . . Well, actually, he didn't have time to finish thinking about it because his shell was now so hot that he couldn't really think at all.

His thinking wasn't much better when Jake pulled him out of the water about three minutes later. Jake, Brody, and the Rhino2000 had given up on the room with the green glow and busted down Punching Crab's door instead. And it was just in time. Punching Crab was still alive. But his shell was burning, and his beady eyes were blank.

"Punch, Punch," yelled Jake, holding him up in the air. "Please, talk to me." Then he added, "Or talk to Brody."

It's hard to know exactly what Punch was trying to articulate, but this is what he said: "My tricycle was stolen by donkey boots." And it didn't make any more sense when Brody translated.

"The red pepper hankered down the blueberry bucket," Punching Crab added. "And don't forget the tartar sauce."

"He'll be fine," said Felonious, after he gave his old friend a brief checkup. "His brain is just a little overheated. It'll take a few days to cool down again. But he'll be back to normal in no time."

Jake gently laid Punching Crab across the Rhino2000's dashboard, while Brody turned to the Fish Doctor with a biting glare, and the Fish Doctor knew exactly what he was implying.

"Hey, I tried to warn him," claimed the Fish Doctor.

"Well, you didn't do a very good job," Brody responded.

"Do I even know you?" asked the Fish Doctor. "Who do

you think you are?"

"I think I'm the guy who's trying to save the last Akaway."

"By leading the fishnappers right to me?" argued the Fish Doctor. "Was that part of your master plan?"

"You're blaming us for this?" yelled Brody.

"Who else am I going to blame?"

"Well, certainly not Punch. If it weren't for him, we would never have come for you."

"Then you'd never know how to open the portal to Sarraka," answered the Fish Doctor.

"You're a lying fish fillet!" yelled Brody, taking a step closer to the fish.

"You're a delusional little brat!" yelled the Fish Doctor, who instinctively positioned his fins in a karate pose.

"The cantaloupe got married to the artichoke with cotton balls," added Punching Crab.

It might have been the word *cotton* or more likely the word *balls*, but when he heard it repeated over and over, the Fish Doctor couldn't help but smile. And we already know smiles are contagious, so Brody smiled too, and after the whole conversation was translated for Jake, he smiled as well.

"I'll put my fins down if you do," said the Fish Doctor, and they both did.

There were a few more seconds of heavy breathing before the Fish Doctor finally showed just a little spark of the old Felonious.

"I guess we have a lot to talk about," he said.

"I guess we do," agreed Brody.

That was Jake's cue to fire up the Rhino2000. He then transformed the wall behind the hot tub into a doorway of splinters. Noticing that the balcony wasn't going to hold up much longer, Jake reached under the lawn mower and pulled out a rope with a strong hook known as a carabiner.

"Here," he said, passing the supplies to Brody. "Hook the carabiner onto the railing. Take Punching Crab and the Fish Doctor, and go."

Brody heard the balcony start to creak.

"What are you going to do?" he asked Jake.

"Don't worry about me," Jake answered. "I'll meet you on the other side of the ramp. Hurry, this thing's about to break."

Jake reversed the lawn mower back into the room,

securing the balcony for enough time to allow Brody to rappel down, with the Fish Doctor and Punching Crab resting comfortably in his hood.

Wincing from the pain in his shoulder, Jake waited until he was sure the rest of the gang was safe. Then, just before the support beams started to burst and the balcony started to fall, he headed toward the hole in the wall, which would have put the finishing touches on a perfect escape had it not been for the big, fat, and surprisingly fast pig that showed up behind him.

"Oink, oink, oink, oink, oink," said Gizmo, which clearly meant, "You're not going anywhere, big boy." He pointed his pig hooves to his eyes and then to Jake, and we all know what that means.

"You've got to be kidding me," Jake said, rolling his eyes.

Jake rubbed his shoulder. He remembered the toll his body took during his first encounter with this pig and knew he couldn't take it again in his current state. He dashed toward the balcony but froze when he noticed it was starting to collapse. Understanding Jake was wounded and had nowhere to run, Gizmo smirked and slowly crept toward him. It was in the menacing smirk that Jake started to realize what Uncle Skeeta was talking about. *This is about more than video games. It's about making dreams come true*, he thought to himself. And it was clear now that fighting might be his only option.

Sequestered
Spring

"Where is he?" worried Brody, who felt like he had been waiting on the safe side of the fence for half of forever.

"I'm sure he'll be fine," comforted the Fish Doctor, placing his fin around Brody's shoulder. "Ocelots don't die easy. Just try to relax. You don't look so good."

"I don't feel so good," said Brody, plopping down against the fence.

"Let me take a look."

Felonious moved closer to Brody, who allowed the Fish Doctor to inspect the cut above his eye.

"You really are the one," whispered the Fish Doctor

in awe. He looked up at Brody and, raising his voice just a little, declared, "You must be a remarkable young man if you've been trusted to have the power of the Akaway."

"I don't know how much power I have left," admitted Brody. The Fish Doctor patted the cut softly and, in a more doctor-sounding voice, said, "Well, we'll have to get you stronger if you're going to hike down to the Sequestered Spring in time for the Illumination."

"Sequestered Spring? Illumination?" repeated Brody. "What are you talking about?"

"You know what I'm talking about," replied the Fish Doctor. "It's what you've been looking for. What we've all been looking for. It's the way to open the portal to Sarraka. It can only be done at the Sequestered Spring on the day of the Illumination."

"What's an Illumination?" asked Brody.

"It's tough to explain. But basically, it's kind of like a sharp burst of light that is like nothing you've ever seen or experienced," described Felonious. "Talk about power: It can make you stronger or it can destroy you. But it's the only way to open the portal. If you're successful, the portal will remain open for exactly six minutes. That's how much time it will take for the perfect amount of energy to flow between the two worlds. But if you fail, the portal will be locked forever."

No pressure, thought Brody, still leaning pathetically against the fence.

"So when is it?" he asked. "When is the Illumination?"

"If the legend is correct," said Felonious, "in seven days."

Brody counted on his fingers. His eyes widened.

"But that's my birthday," he said.

"Of course it is," said Felonious. "It has to be. That's when your powers are the strongest."

"What are you talking about?" asked Brody, his mind still groggy.

"It's called a birthday party," said Felonious. "I'm sure you've heard of them."

Brody had heard of them. He just had never had one. That was one of the problems with having a birthday at the end of December. Most kids were either out of town or with relatives for the holidays. So Brody spent all his birthdays with Grammy, and he never once complained.

"How in the world is a birthday party going to help me?" said Brody.

"Friends," said Felonious. "Your power will increase with more friends around you."

Jake could have used a few friends as he danced around the room, trying to absorb the multiple attacks from Gizmo. Knocked down again and again by the incredible force of a charging pig, Jake somehow managed to keep getting up, but his shoulder was too weak to fight back in any meaningful way.

"Oink, oink, oink," bellowed Gizmo, and by now Jake could pretty much understand that he meant, "Playtime is over, big boy. It's time to finish you off—pig style."

In desperation, Jake scanned the room for something, anything he could use as a weapon or a shield to protect his right shoulder. That's when he saw the platform above the hot tub. The one that looked like a snowboard. Jake took a few quick steps to his right, ripped the platform free, and placed his good arm through the two leather loops that secured it to the stand in the first place.

Jake swung the platform through the air, daring Gizmo to come closer. Gizmo froze, calculating his next move. But Jake had already planned his. Those leather loops were pretty good on his arm, but Jake decided they would be better on his feet, so he dropped the platform to the ground.

"Time to start shredding the gnar," Jake said, which is one way to say, "We're going snowboarding." He darted for fresh air and placed his feet on the board. The balcony was hanging down at the perfect angle for a 50/50 grind, so that's what Jake did. Gizmo rushed to the edge, but he could only watch as Jake turned the perfect sledding hill into the perfect shredding hill. Aided by the balance and coordination of an ocelot, Jake straight-lined right down the hill, gaining more and more speed, until he hit the escape jump. That's when he pulled a backside rodeo and landed safely on the other side of the fence, where Brody, Felonious, and Punching Crab were waiting.

"Wow," said Felonious. "That's quite a relationship you have with your spirit animal."

"You really think so?" Jake beamed after Brody translated. "I'm an ocelot. We fight to the death." Jake glanced down at his snowboard, before adding, "And sometimes we run for our lives."

"Well, either way," said Felonious. "I'm glad I'm on your side."

The curtains in the front of the house just barely opened. Peering out were the ocean-blue eyes of Uncle Skeeta and the dark brown eyes of Gizmo. What they saw was Jake with his throbbing shoulder, Brody with his worn-out spirit, Punching Crab with his boiled brain, and the Fish Doctor, who surprisingly seemed just fine—ambling safely down the path. Uncle Skeeta glanced down as if to say, "They think they've won the battle, but let's see if they're ready for the war."

That Beautiful Sweet Glow

When you can't participate in the kind of adventures you've embraced your entire life, sometimes the best nourishment for your wounded spirit is hearing all about those adventures from those who can. So even though Grammy was weak and tired, she demanded every last detail about Jake and Brody Boondoggle's latest adventure, right down to the details about the Sequestered Spring and the spit that opened the secret door.

"Oh my great grandfather from Grenada with grilled banana-split dump cake, orange marmalade topping, and fluted cinnamon jelly beans," said Grammy, with the Akaway lying beside her on the water bed—its breathing still constant, but noticeably weaker. "That certainly sounds like an amazing door."

"Yeah," said Jake, with a combination of admiration and concern. "Talk about impossible to open."

"Oh, nothing's impossible," said Grammy. "You'd be surprised at the doors you can open simply by keeping an open mind."

Jake nodded, but Brody didn't respond. His mind was clearly not open, and it took a couple of tries before he answered Grammy when she asked, "And how are you feeling now?"

"Like I have no energy," admitted Brody, and he felt the same way for the next several days.

"The Fish Doctor said this would happen, but nobody expected it to be this bad," explained Jake.

Brody was tired. Too tired to change his clothes. Too tired to go outside. Even too tired to hike back for spirit-animal training with the Fish Doctor and Punching Crab, despite Jake's constant urging.

The reality was that, for the first time in his life, Brody was too tired to do anything except. . . . "I'll just play video games," he said, which was exactly what he had done most of his waking hours for the last couple days.

It took Jake that long to see a *human* doctor about his shoulder, which was not broken, just bruised, and was actually starting to feel better. It wasn't much longer before his body was healing, his spirit was willing, and his mind was focused on his promise to Grammy. It was just five days before Brody's birthday, and there wasn't any more time to waste.

"Come on," said Jake, bursting into the guest room. "We gotta get going."

"Get going where?" asked Brody, without diverting his eyes from the screen.

"Are you joking?" said Jake, his eyes shifting to the video game. Jake quickly shook his head free and spoke with appropriate outrage. "We have to meet with the Fish Doctor. You know: Help you get stronger. Find the Sequestered Spring. Save the Akaway. Just little unimportant things like that."

That's when Jake got a taste of what selective hearing felt like. Brody ignored him, and Jake didn't like it one bit. He grabbed the controller from Brody's hands.

"Hey, what are you doing?" yelled Brody.

"The question is, 'What are *you* doing?'" Jake shot back.

"I'm in the middle of a mission right now," said Brody. He grabbed the video game back from Jake and was instantly reengaged. Brody could sense Jake watching as he operated the controls like a seasoned professional. He knew Jake loved video games, and, in most cases, it was Jake who woke up and flipped on the game without even thinking of other options. So Brody didn't need the help of any spirit animal to think of this idea.

"Why don't you join me?" he said in a soft, inviting voice with his eyebrows elevated. An alluring grin appeared on his face. "It's cold outside. You hear that wind? It's telling us to stay inside today. Your shoulder is barely healed. It needs a little more rest. We'll get to all that other stuff later. I promise." He felt the cut above his left eye and showed Jake the small residue of blood. "See that? We have time. Let's just stay in and play. Come on. This'll be fun."

Brody didn't wait for an answer. Instead, he kept playing, skillfully providing the game's hero with the power of a wolverine so he could climb the impossible hill and advance to Stage Two of an ingenious game that Uncle Skeeta had created. Jake took a moment to watch Brody, who was actually getting pretty good. The truth was that a significant part of Jake was tempted to grab some kind of cereal with sugar as its first ingredient, cuddle back down under a few toasty blankets, and work all day side by side with his brother until the mission was complete.

Back and forth the struggle for Jake's spirit went. On one end was an ocelot, tugging and twisting and leaning back with all its weight trying to pull Jake outside. But on the other side was the video game, armed with hypnotizing images geared specifically to kids just like Jake and Brody, encouraging him to relax, take it easy, stay cozy warm, and enjoy.

Jake shook his head, vigorously trying to free himself from that beautiful, sweet glow of the video game console. Maybe he would have done it by himself, but we'll never know. Because at that moment, someone—or something— scurried over to the television set, grabbed the plug, and yanked.

Love and Laughter and Lollygagging

Nothingness filled the screen, and when Brody's eyes brightened just slightly, Punching Crab, with the cord in his claw, could see just a small sliver of spirit return. He nodded to Jake, who stuck out his hand, and Brody grabbed it. Candy wrappers, salt-n-vinegar-flavored potato-chip crumbs, and half of a stale French baguette slipped off Brody's lap as he walked to the window and saw large soft flakes of perfectly white snow falling from the sky.

"You're going to be better in no time," said Punching Crab. "You just need to get back to basics."

It took a little longer than normal, but soon enough, Brody was dressed and on his way out the door. That's when he banged right into Rudy. The impact knocked his best friend off the steps, over the railing, and into the bushes.

"Sorry, Rudacious," said Brody, helping him up. "Wrong time. Wrong place."

"Where are you going?" asked Rudy, showing a little frustration as he dusted off his jacket. "I thought we were hanging out."

"We are," said Brody. "We're just hanging out outside."

"That's not what you said when you invited me over," argued Rudy. "You said we were going to beat that video game."

"Go for it," interjected Jake, who trusted his instincts and hid Punching Crab in his jacket. "But we have more important things to do."

Rudy looked to Brody, hoping for the support that he never had to worry about before. But this time, like the last time, it didn't come—although Brody repeated the invitation for Rudy to join them outside.

"That wasn't the plan," said Rudy, hunching up his shoulders as he felt the cold wind blow. "I'm out of here."

For a few steps, Brody tried to talk Rudy into staying, but then the extraordinary powers of nature took over.

Brody's eyes widened as he took it all in. The world was a clean slate. No footprints. No tire or animal tracks. Everything was fresh, clean, and possible. And trying to get Rudy to change his mind just didn't seem as important.

"Ahh," said Brody, the cool air filling his nose and lungs with every breath. Immediately, Jake and Punching Crab could see the spirit in Brody growing stronger.

"Take another deep breath," Punching Crab instructed. "In fact, take five."

Brody did.

"How do you feel?" Punching Crab asked.

"Better."

"Well, the red table just swarmed past the beehive with a big mug of jellyfish," said Punching Crab. He fell back, grabbed a snowball, and placed it on his head. "Sorry," he said. "I'm not quite a hundred percent yet. But Felonious says it shouldn't be much longer."

"Where is the Fish Doctor?" asked Brody.

"He's waiting for you to get stronger so the purple pumpkin can get to the store before the teapot goes reindeer."

After Brody translated, Jake helped Punch to the side of the yard where he could just sit and relax. "That's okay,"

Jake said softly. "Don't worry about a thing. I'll take over from here. You just get better."

And when Punching Crab watched what happened next, he did.

Jake walked over to the empty lot next to Grammy's, and immediately Brody knew exactly what Jake was thinking. He should have known because it was his idea in the first place. In the lot, there was a hill, almost like a ramp. Just off the end of the hill was a tree, and on one of the branches Brody had tied a rope. He had gotten the idea after learning that orangutans can travel for miles in the rain forest without ever touching the ground. If the snow was collecting fast enough, like it was right now, you could run up this ramp at full speed, dive for the rope like an experienced orangutan, swing over the wooden fence—which you obviously pretended were the teeth of a prehistoric Tyrannosaurus rex—and land safely on the other side.

"Doodle sack," Jake yelled as he snagged the rope with his good arm and started to swing across the fence. He spun in the air, pretending to avoid poisonous darts, and landed on his feet. Brody watched Jake do it again and again and again, each time yelling something just a little odd for no good reason other than to make himself smile.

"Bindle stiff."

"Pukester."

"Bunghole." (Which is not a bad word like some people may think. It's actually a hole for emptying a keg or barrel.)

Finally, Jake walked over and gave Brody a friendly shove, if there is such a thing that can come from a big brother.

"Come on, Brody. Your turn," he said. "You can do it."

Brody walked over hesitantly, got a running start, and took off.

"Vanilla!" he yelled as he flew through the air. Punching Crab cringed both at Brody's lame choice of funny phrases and also because Brody let go too early and was swallowed up by the Tyrannosaurus rex. *That's gotta hurt*, he thought to himself.

But Jake chose to encourage Brody instead of criticizing him.

"It's a start," he said. "Now do it again."

"Watching paint dry!" yelled Brody just before another less-than-graceful dismount.

"Seeing grass grow."

"Homework on the weekends."

When Brody yelled out, "Brush your teeth before bed," Jake had heard enough.

"Come on now, you can do better than that," he said. "Stop thinking so much. You're an orangutan," said Jake. "Now don't think. Just be. Be an orangutan."

"You really believe I can do it?" asked Brody.

"I keep telling you," said Jake. "It doesn't matter what I believe. It doesn't matter what Grammy believes. It doesn't matter what Punching Crab or the Fish Doctor or the Akaway or anyone else believes. It only matters what you believe. And when you finally realize that, then you'll find the magic again."

Brody started backing up slowly, step by step, thinking less and less about what Jake had just said and more and more about getting an extra long start to his next jump.

I'm an orangutan, he told himself, and then he made himself believe it.

"Winklepicker."

"Nudiustertian."

"Tittynope." (Don't let yourself get in trouble for this one either. It simply means a small quantity of anything left over—like sweet potatoes on your dinner plate.)

Time flew by quickly as Brody gained more and more confidence with every jump. It always does when your spirit is thriving, and the next few days were filled with love and laughter and lollygagging. There were snowball fights and fort building, sledding and snowboarding, and, of course, a steady diet of snow cones, which sadly are rarely ever made anymore with real snow like they should be.

As Brody got stronger, he started working with Felonious to prepare for all the potential questions, problems, and complications surrounding the upcoming mission. Felonious taught Brody elite spirit-animal skills, such as belly breathing, which is used to make your body powerful, calm, and centered. He helped Brody learn to read auras to evaluate people by their actions instead of their words. He showed Brody how he could use his extraordinary new instincts to find the Sequestered Spring. They even created invitations for the first birthday party of Brody's life and delivered them to every kid who was still around.

When they were done, Felonious steered Brody over to a snowbank, sat him down, and told him something he never dreamed he would say.

"You're ready."

Realizations

It felt as if the sun were rising just for Brody Boondoggle, and his eyes sprang open at the exact moment it peeked over the horizon. He didn't even think about the dream, even though he had it again the night before. All his senses were heightened, meaning they were stronger than ever before. He could see more clearly, hear more acutely, touch more precisely, taste more perceptively, and smell more intensely. There was no doubt. He was now at his most powerful.

Today was his birthday.

And although this birthday was sure to be unlike any he had ever experienced, he wanted to start the celebration in the exact way he had done ever since he could remember. So he climbed out of his bed and rushed up to Grammy's room.

Had this been like any other birthday, Grammy would have been snoring like a locomotive. When she finally awoke, she would pull out the plan and all the supplies for their all-day adventure. One year, they needed to track down the diabolical Black Tooth who had stolen all his presents. Another, he had to earn back his birthday cake by proving his strength and courage against the Evil Cake Master. And on another, they simply hiked down to the open field for an intense snowball fight, followed by a fort- and snowman-building competition.

But Brody didn't expect any of that from Grammy this year. He knew she was too weak, and he was content to slowly creep in, check on the Akaway, and lie quietly with Grammy for a couple minutes. Unfortunately, there was one small problem with that plan. When Brody opened the door, Grammy was gone.

When you have the powers of an Akaway, and you happen to be at your strongest, tracking down an aging and ill Grammy is not really a challenge, so Brody had little trouble finding Grammy walking slowly down the path into the woods. She moved tentatively, which means the spring in her step was completely gone.

Just for fun, Brody secretly followed Grammy farther and farther into the woods. The fun ended when he finally realized that she was heading to the house on the top of a hill—the one that was perfect for sledding.

But now, the peeling white paint and ominous black shutters were covered by a big, colorful electronic sign that read: *Rudy's Birthday Party Extravaganza*.

So focused on the sign was Brody that he didn't notice soft footsteps sneaking up behind him.

"Are you here for the party?"

Those words startled Brody almost as much as the sign, and he spun around to see his best friend looking right at him. "I mean, I was planning to invite you," continued Rudy. "But you didn't seem to have the time."

Rudy didn't normally have parties for the same reason that Brody didn't, but he explained that this year, his uncle had insisted. This same uncle offered to plan and host the festivities, and he wouldn't take no for an answer.

"I guess you're not coming to my party," said Brody.

"I guess not," replied Rudy, with a little edge in his voice. "I've got my own."

He handed Brody a long, cylindrical container, holding what seemed like a pair of regular sunglasses. Unless you knew they weren't. "Put them on," instructed Rudy.

Brody stood frozen, staring at the sunglasses. He recognized these sunglasses from the lake with the hunter.

"Go ahead," Rudy said quietly. "They're really cool."

So Brody did, and what happened next was more than cool. There were three-dimensional animals, and lasers, and fireworks, all promoting *Rudy's Birthday Party Extravaganza*, "where a brand-new video game will be debuted." A cold chill crept down Brody's spine. He pulled the glasses from his face.

"Let me ask you something," he said. "This uncle of yours. What's his name?"

Of course Brody knew the answer. But it didn't seem real until Rudy raised his head to look Brody right in the eye. "You mean Uncle Skeeta?"

Brody closed his eyes, shook his head, and took a deep breath. "Now let me ask you something else," he said. "When I called you about the Akaway, you asked me where I saw it, and I told you. Did you tell anyone else?"

"Yeah," said Rudy.

"Who?"

"Uncle Skeeta."

We Have a Deal

Brody slowly handed the sunglasses back to Rudy, now knowing that the meeting at the lake with the "hunter" was no coincidence. He turned his head to see Grammy waiting at the big red door. Seconds later, Uncle Skeeta appeared. He kissed Grammy on the cheek and welcomed her inside before closing the door behind her.

"It's been too long," said Uncle Skeeta, in that special way that makes everyone feel like Uncle Skeeta's best friend. But, in this case, Grammy was.

Or, she used to be.

But that was a long time ago, when Uncle Skeeta was still trying to figure out what to do with his life. Grammy had been immediately drawn to his brilliant sense of humor and his willingness to laugh at himself; his ability to connect to children, men, and women of all ages; his readiness to fight for what he believed in; and his generosity and kindness for those who couldn't fight for themselves. Not to mention his great love of animals.

So Grammy taught him a new way of looking at the world, described the legend of the Akaway, and connected him to his spirit animal. And Uncle Skeeta soaked it all in. Embraced it, mastered it, and then used all he had learned to create the kind of games that kids couldn't resist.

"It's such a pleasure to have you here," he said, and he meant it, even if it was still a little awkward hosting the woman whom he had so totally betrayed. Then, as if he had been expecting her, he handed Grammy a warm cup of tea and pulled out a plate of sticky cinnamon rolls with chocolate cream-cheese icing.

"This is delicious," Grammy said, taking several bites of her cinnamon roll.

"I learned from the best. Please have another." And Grammy did.

"I see you're having a party," said Grammy, observing the setup.

"As are you," countered Uncle Skeeta.

"Oh, it's not me," corrected Grammy. "And that brings me to the reason for my visit." She looked Uncle Skeeta right in the eye. "I know you well enough to know that you're not going to change your plans because of me. And I would never ask you to be someone you're not. But I do have a proposition for you." Grammy paused for a moment. "How about we stay out of this?"

"What do you mean?" asked Uncle Skeeta.

"I mean, this is about the kids. So let's let them decide how it works out," said Grammy. "Without any interference from us."

Uncle Skeeta leaned back and crossed his legs, pondering Grammy's proposal.

"Are you telling me you'd leave something as important as this strictly up to a bunch of children?" he whispered into Grammy's good ear. Uncle Skeeta stood up and paced around before sitting back down. "You have a lot of confidence in these kids," he continued. "We've seen what happens when children are left to their own devices."

"Unfortunately, we don't get to see that enough," said Grammy. "I say we let them fail or succeed on their own."

"And what if they fail?"

"They pick themselves up and figure out what to do next," said Grammy. "Or they don't. But let's give them that chance. What a great birthday gift that would be, don't you think?"

"And what about Felonious and the Crab?"

"They're just along for the ride," promised Grammy.

"But look at all the work I've already done," said Uncle Skeeta. "I'll need to get the kids started. Explain everything. Answer any questions they might have."

"That seems reasonable," said Grammy.

She collected a large volume of saliva in her mouth, turned her back slightly, and appeared to spit into her right hand. Then Grammy held out her hand. "Do we have a deal?"

The truth was Uncle Skeeta was going to say yes all along. He could never say no to Grammy. After all, she never said no to him.

"Okay," he said, performing the same ritual by spitting into his hand. "We have a deal."

It was the same way Grammy and Uncle Skeeta had sealed their agreements since the first time they met— when Uncle Skeeta officially swore to protect all the secrets of Sarraka. When the handshake was done, Grammy secretly closed her fist and smiled. Then she took a step closer to Uncle Skeeta, kissed him on the cheek, and walked right out the front door, keeping the saliva safely in her hand the entire time.

That Little Voice

Grammy tried her hardest to hike home with a clear conscience, knowing she had no control over the person Uncle Skeeta had become, so she tried not to think about it. Instead she enjoyed what she could control. She called on her sixth sense to embrace all that was still connected in nature. She viewed the world through her third eye to see all the different and complex auras that combined to make us who we were. And she reveled in the magic and fantasy of her surroundings and all the amazing potential they offered for birthday adventures like the one in store for Brody Boondoggle.

Her soul was at peace, and although her instincts were still fading, they were as sharp now, in her element, as they possibly could be. And that meant they were sharp enough to notice when she was being followed.

"Are you ready to come out now and join me?" she called into the air. Then she stopped and turned around. "It's okay. It's kind of a tradition."

That's when Brody Boondoggle emerged from behind a great oak tree. Grammy just smiled and continued her leisurely stroll while Brody hurried to catch up.

"How'd you know I was there?" asked Brody.

"Oh, I know that you care," replied Grammy. "You're just kind of moody sometimes. You know, selfish. Like you only think about yourself. But I'm sure you'll figure it out."

It was starting to feel like a normal birthday, and it would have been easy for Brody to forget about his meeting with Rudy and Grammy's visit to Uncle Skeeta's, but he couldn't.

"What were you thinking?" yelled Brody.

Grammy stopped in her tracks and then turned to face Brody. She thought for a second before responding with,

"Now why would you ask that?"

"Oh, I don't know," replied Brody sarcastically. "Maybe because that guy you just met with shot the Akaway."

Grammy looked at him and took a deep breath. "The Akaway is a wise creature," she said. "Remember, everything happens for a reason."

"What possible reason could there be?" responded Brody.

"I can't answer that," said Grammy. "That's your journey."

She looked all around, reinvigorated by her surroundings, which means that nature actually made her feel better, if only for this walk. The sun was bright and the wind mild, making the cold temperatures for this time of year feel reasonable.

"Somebody must be looking out for you," she said, trying to subtly change the subject. "You couldn't have a nicer day for your party."

"I want you to be there with me," said Brody. "I want it to be like it always is."

"Oh, my love," she said. "I would love to spend your birthday with you, just the way we have every year. But this year is different. This is a big birthday in so many ways, and I can't go with you the way I used to. Not this year."

"Then I should stay home with you," said Brody, tears forming in his eyes.

"Oh, and nothing would make me happier," said Grammy, wiping his eyes with the end of her homemade purple scarf. "It would be perfect for you to stay home with me. We could talk about magic and spirits and tell crazy stories all through the day. But what about the Akaway? Listen to me carefully. You have so much more in you, and it can't grow and thrive if you stay inside with me all day. Especially not on your birthday. Not this birthday. The Akaway needs you." Then she picked his chin up and looked him in the eye. "And so do I."

Grammy paused and just looked at Brody—all of 12 years old now, already wise beyond his years in so many ways and yet with so much to learn. There was so much still to tell him.

"What?" Brody finally said, feeling uneasy under the weight of Grammy's gaze.

But this was not the time, so, instead, Grammy focused on what she loved best. "Besides," she answered. "While you're away on another adventure, I'll have time to prepare the special, super-duper, double-ripple, hot fudge, chocolate pudding birthday cake that we'll share when you've opened the portal to Sarraka and saved the Akaway."

"You'll be there when we do?" asked Brody.

Grammy just smiled and said, "Yes."

Part III
The Reflection

chapter 36

The Mutiny vs. The Eliminators

"Welcome, welcome, welcome," said Uncle Skeeta, with a warm smile and a twinkle in his eyes. He was standing in front of the big TV in his game room, addressing all the kids attending *Rudy's Birthday Party Extravaganza*.

There was Lainey, who was so excited to attend Rudy's party that she literally jumped out of her dad's car before it had come to a complete stop. Geovanny set all the clocks in his house ahead by 15 minutes to trick his parents into dropping him off early, so his little sister, Kai, was forced to go early as well. Cole had nagged, "Are we there yet?" over and over to make his mom drive faster, which actually worked. And Brian and Jared took matters into their own hands by riding their bikes—in the snow—so they wouldn't be late.

Uncle Skeeta planned for all the kids in the neighborhood to attend, which would have left none for Brody's party. And it would have worked too, but. . . .

Jaylan lied about being sick so he wouldn't have to take his social studies test. The problem was he seemed fine for basketball practice later that night. Jaylan was grounded. Three weeks without video games. For some reason, Alec accepted a dare to drink out of the school's toilet. He was punished with a mouthful of soap and two weeks of no video games. Halil was furious with his big sister, Imani, for starting a rumor that he had a girlfriend. But it probably wasn't such a good idea to get even by giving her a faux-hawk in the middle of the night. That little stunt was rewarded with a month of no video games.

Ranjeta volunteered at the local library. Occasionally, Brody would see her there, and they would talk about school, or books, or Brody's recurring dream about the waterslide, the lock, and the unreachable key that was buried deep down in a hole. Ranjeta was fascinated by dreams. One day Ranjeta thought it would be pretty funny to freak out her grandfather by sabotaging his library books. She secretly hid an electronic surveillance strip in each binding and placed one strategically in the bottom of his backpack. When her grandfather tried to leave the library, the alarm went off, and, just like that, he was known throughout the community as the Library Book Bandit. When the truth came out, Ranjeta was grounded. No video games for a month.

And then there was Bonita, who was known at school for two things: being tough and being just a little bit different—kind of like Brody. She was never punished at all. But something felt right about Brody's party. So when she was invited, she said, "I'll be there." At least that's what she meant when she punched him in the chest. Another punch meant she agreed to bring her little brother Felix.

Most of these kids weren't particularly excited about Brody's party, especially when there was a better option going on. The kids at the better option, on the other hand, were already cheering as Uncle Skeeta announced, "Are you ready for the world premiere of a video game that will change the universe?" He paused appropriately for the cheers to get even louder before adding, "Then let's get this party started."

With that, all the kids at Rudy's party strapped themselves securely into their very own, form-fitted game chairs and placed custom-made helmets on their heads. They sat in front of a high-definition screen as Uncle Skeeta pulled a remote control from his holster, aimed it at the TV, and clicked the power button.

A ray of light burst from the monitor. The combination of graphics, music, and lights was unlike anything the kids had ever experienced. The TV seemed almost alive. Reading their thoughts, anticipating their desires, manipulating every aspect of Uncle Skeeta's latest video game just for them. It was the future of video games, right now.

"Now that my latest creation has your attention," Uncle Skeeta said proudly, "let me explain to you how this is going to work."

Uncle Skeeta used laser pointers, three-dimensional charts, and a brief video to tell the kids all about the Sequestered Spring, the Illumination, and the portal to Sarraka.

"In this game, there are two worlds," described Uncle

Skeeta. "Our world and Sarraka. Now, there is a group of misguided children who want to combine these two worlds by opening a portal, or a doorway, so they can save some animal called an Akaway."

"What's an Akaway?" asked Lainey.

Uncle Skeeta couldn't resist. "Oh, about 50 pounds," he replied. Then after waiting just enough time for the kids to figure out the joke and smile, Uncle Skeeta quickly clarified, "It's just a crazy animal that you've never heard of."

"So what's wrong with saving it?" asked Kai innocently, her little legs dangling off the chair.

"I'll tell you what's wrong," said Uncle Skeeta. "Those kids are the bad guys, that's what's wrong." He pointed to one side of a chart that showed images of all the kids at Brody's party: Brody, Jake, Alec, Halil, Jaylan, Ranjeta, Bonita, and Felix. "This group of bad guys will be known as The Mutiny."

"Why The Mutiny?" asked Kai.

"Because that's what you call a group of people who rebel against their leaders," explained Uncle Skeeta. "And that's what these guys are doing."

"But aren't those kids our friends?" asked Cole, with a

warm smile.

"Great question," responded Uncle Skeeta. "Just so we're clear, the kids in the game aren't real. I just used the names and images to make it a little more fun. Remember, this is just a game. It's a very special game that will make impossible things seem to happen right before your eyes. But no matter how real it seems, you must always remember that these things are only happening on the screen. You got it?"

All heads nodded up and down.

"Very good," said Uncle Skeeta. He pushed a big red button on his belt, and, instantly, everyone received frosty mugs filled with root beer milk shakes.

"Now the way to connect these two worlds is through this portal right here," continued Uncle Skeeta. He pointed to a round object that looked like an oversized electric fan. "The portal can only be opened in one place, at one moment in time. The time is called the Illumination, and the place is called the Sequestered Spring. Your goal is stop The Mutiny from reaching the Sequestered Spring in time for the Illumination. If you win, the portal will disappear, and you will be the heroes who saved the world. If you lose, The Mutiny wins, and the world as you know it might never be the same."

"Don't worry, we got this," yelled a dark-haired kid with jeans and a "Let's Rock" T-shirt.

"What's your name?" said Uncle Skeeta.

"Geovanny, dude."

Uncle Skeeta smiled and said, "I like you, kid," before getting back to his presentation. He pointed to the wall where there was what appeared to be an ordinary traffic light, except that it contained four lights instead of three. In addition to the regular red, yellow, and green, there was also an orange light.

"There are four stages of this game," said Uncle Skeeta. "Right now, The Mutiny is just getting ready to start its hike to the Sequestered Spring, so The Mutiny is at Stage 1: Red. If they get closer, they will advance to Stage 2, or yellow. Then Stage 3, or green. And if they get to Stage 4, orange, they have successfully reached the Sequestered Spring in time for the Illumination to open the portal to Sarraka."

"Can we stop them with kung fu?" asked Brian, a 12-year-old boy wearing a red "I'm in charge here" T-shirt. "I want to be a kung fu fighter."

"No kung fu," said Uncle Skeeta. "But we will have plenty of tools at our disposal—you'll learn more about that when the game starts. If we are successful, and a member of The Mutiny is eliminated, he or she will be removed from the board. Once all the names are removed, or if they don't get to the Sequestered Spring in time, you win. Everyone understand?"

Uncle Skeeta took the chanting of "We wanna play, we wanna play," as a yes. He then pointed to a giant timer located on the bottom right-hand corner of the enormous screen on the wall. It read Illumination, and, according to the time, the Illumination was to occur in 2 hours, 59 minutes and 13, 12, 11, 10, 9, 8 seconds.

"Will you be here to help if we need you?" asked Jared, whose runner's build and light brown hair down to his shoulders made him appear younger than his actual age of 13.

Uncle Skeeta didn't hesitate. "Of course I will," he said with a smile. "You're not alone. Just ring your ringer, and I'll be right in to help in any way I can." There was a brief pause as he and Rudy exchanged a look that was difficult to define, but definitely worth noting.

"I have a question," said Brian. "What's our team name?"

"That's a good question," replied Uncle Skeeta. "Any ideas?"

Suggestions ranged from The Ashmonsters to The Zombies, but nothing seemed right until Geovanny yelled out, "How about The Eliminators?"

"The Eliminators," repeated Uncle Skeeta. "The Mutiny versus The Eliminators. I like it."

The *B* Word

Things weren't quite as exciting at the start of Brody Boondoggle's birthday party. Brody didn't have lasers or graphics or super electronics. There wasn't a bubble maker, a chocolate fountain, or even the personalized toilet paper.

Brody simply explained the whole story about the Akaway, the portal, and Sarraka, and then announced, "We're going to find the Sequestered Spring."

"Does that even exist?" asked Bonita, who had heard similar stories from her grandfather. "I thought it was just a legend."

"I guess we'll find out," said Brody.

He handed each guest an ordinary gray backpack, filled with all the supplies a kid might need for an adventure to a distant, magical destination.

"That's it?" questioned Felix, in the kind of voice 7-year-olds use when you know they don't want to try something new. "Hiking to find an imaginary place that doesn't exist?"

But that wasn't all he said. In his next sentence, he dropped the *B* word.

"This is boring," Felix repeated. "I'm bored just think-ing about it."

"What did he just say?" cringed Punching Crab, and Felonious repeated the only word that caused Punching Crab to lose his cool. In fact, if you asked anyone who had ever been connected to the spirit-animal world in any way, they'd all tell you the same thing: There is nothing more disturbing than a healthy child with the ability to run, jog, skip, gallop, sprint, hop, lope, scamper, jump, bound, leap, soar, swim, dart, buzz, dash, dance, boogie, salsa, bop, chant, whistle, sing, hum, imagine, explore, in-vestigate, interpret, analyze, envision, visualize, consider, read, build, doodle, craft, construct, draw, sketch, observe, think, scribble, examine, create, distinguish, portray, train, comprehend, illustrate, study, sense, joke, evaluate, feel, experience, and dream who still claimed, as Felix did, "I'm bored."

"I'm going to rip that kid's tongue out and beat him with it," whispered Punching Crab. "Hold me back," he whispered before yelling, "Let me at him!"

While Brody was dealing with the Felix situation, Jake heard a soft voice in a spirited tone. It was Grammy asking Jake very nicely to come inside and see her, just as she had 13 days earlier.

When Jake entered Grammy's room, she was lying on the bed. Jake noticed that she looked more tired now, more worn out by the weight of the world, as if she had used her last gasp of energy on the hike to Uncle Skeeta's house.

"Do you need something?" Jake asked. "Is everything okay?"

Grammy sat up weakly and motioned to a plain white box about the size of a ruler sitting on the dresser.

"Do you want me to give this to Brody?" Jake asked, assuming it was a birthday present.

"No," said Grammy. "This one's for you. Go ahead and open it."

When Jake did, his eyes widened and his jaw dropped.

"Is this what I think it is?" he asked.

Grammy nodded. "Just in case," she said. "Do you know what to do with it?"

"I think so," said Jake. Then he looked up. "Do you really think it will work?"

"You'll have to let me know," said Grammy.

A confident smile formed on Jake's face as he realized exactly what Grammy had done, and what this new gift would mean to the rest of his day. Grammy motioned for him to come closer.

"No matter what happens today," she whispered. "Thank you. You kept your promise. And for that, I will be forever grateful."

Jake covered Grammy with a warm, woolen blanket. "Here's another promise," he whispered. "We're gonna save the Akaway." A small smile appeared as he then spoke to the area where the Akaway lay, even though he couldn't see her. "You hear that, empty jacket? We're gonna save you. So get ready to go home."

Jake placed the box in the inside pocket of his jacket and returned to the party, just in time to see Brody speaking with Felix. A few seconds later, Felix started walking away. When he was completely out of sight, the light that read *Felix* on the video board at Rudy's party went dark.

Thundersnow

The bright sun and mild temperatures left the roads, paths, and trails clear and easy to track; but nothing is easy when you're trying to accomplish something that has never been done before. So Brody wasn't surprised or even upset when his team turned around the very first bend to find "the biggest mountain I've ever seen," proclaimed Jaylan.

"It's just a hill," said Brody. "Let's climb it."

"But it's got no path," complained Jaylan. "It's like no one has ever gone this way before."

"And that's what makes it fun," explained Brody.

Normally, it might be difficult to understand exactly how big the hill was simply by watching television, but this hill was so big that even The Eliminators were in awe.

"I didn't think they made hills that big," said Cole, slurping down the rest of his root beer milk shake. "That can't be climbed."

"Well, let's just make sure of that," said Rudy. "It's time to take some action."

The computer sensed Rudy's meaning and created a menu that allowed his team to choose from 168 different kinds of weather. Everything from acid rain to a zephyr, which is really only a gentle wind, so that didn't seem like a great option. There were tornadoes and hurricanes, mudslides and flash floods, meteor showers and avalanches.

"How about quicksand?" asked Brian.

"Quicksand isn't a kind of weather," said Rudy.

"It could be," said Brian. "We could combine it with a mudslide and call it quickslide so when they slide down the hill, they land in quicksand. That would be sweet."

"I like thundersnow," cried Kai.

"Never heard of it, dude," said Geovanny.

"It's one of the rarest and most powerful kinds of thunderstorms," said Rudy.

He paused, briefly amazed that he could recall a fact

about thundersnow when he was pretty sure he never learned it in the first place. And that's when Rudy realized what Uncle Skeeta knew all along. Brody Boondoggle wasn't the only kid with special powers. Brody and Rudy were connected, and on this day, Rudy felt just a little stronger, and the power felt good.

"That doesn't sound bad enough," said Cole. "I say we go with a tornado, or a flood would be awesome."

"Yeah, dudes, or a hurricane would be pretty intense," said Geovanny.

"I still like thundersnow," repeated Kai, with an adorable little smile.

"C'mon, guys," said Rudy, trying to build support. "How often does anyone ever see thundersnow? Plus, you gotta look at the big picture. Even if it doesn't stop 'em, the rest of the trip will be nearly impossible. All the trails will look the same. They won't know where they're going."

"How about thundersand?" proposed Brian. "So they end up in quicksand."

"There is no quicksand," Rudy reiterated.

"Fine, we can go with thundersnow," agreed Jared. And eventually, every one acquiesced, which is a great word that means agreed to let Kai have her way.

"Okay," said Rudy, winking at Kai. "On the count of three."

The pink and green wires hooked to the temples of The Eliminators' helmets felt warm, but right. The energy passed from their heads to the screen. From there, Rudy took over. His eyes shifted back and forth as if he were watching a tennis match in super speed. Beads of sweat formed on his head. It takes a special kind of energy to transform an idea into reality, and Rudy had it. Soon, The Eliminators were magically transported high into the sky among the clouds. There they hung in the air without wires, without wings, and without support of any kind.

"Is this really happening?" asked Lainey in amazement.

"Remember what Uncle Skeeta said," said Jared. "This game makes impossible things seem real."

"This is amazing," Geovanny said softly after experiencing the magic for the first time.

"Well, let's get going," said Rudy.

"Doing what?" asked Cole.

"Changing the weather, of course. We're going to create thundersnow."

chapter 39

Self-Preservation

B~OOM!~

The Mutiny had only just started climbing from rock to rock when they heard the first sound.

BOOM!

This time, the sound was louder, and it felt like the bolts of lightning were being aimed specifically at the kids climbing the mountain—probably because they were.

BOOM! BOOM!

"What is that?" yelled Ranjeta, covering her ears.

"Thundersnow," Brody said.

"What's thundersnow?"

"It's a rare and powerful kind of thunderstorm,"

answered Brody. Rudy smiled, taking pride in the fact that their minds worked pretty much the same way.

"But it's not snowing," said Alec.

"It will," said Brody and Rudy in unison.

And then it did. With every deafening boom, heavy, dense snowflakes rained from the sky, creating an endless white blanket that smothered everything it touched.

"I can't see," complained Jaylan. "And I can't move either."

Hanging on was even more difficult. Bonita was the first to slip off a rock and fall to the bottom. Soon, Ranjeta followed. Then Alec and Halil.

"Dude, it's working," said Geovanny, watching the scene from his warm, cozy chair. "They're not going to make it."

"If only we had access to quicksand," said Brian.

Rudy ignored that comment, instead focusing on Jake and how the ocelot in him refused to let go. But there was something else. Jake seemed deep in thought. Watching the pace of the snow, listening to the sound of the booms.

"What is it?" asked Brody, who had no problem hanging on, thanks to the climbing power of a mountain goat.

"I don't know," said Jake. "Something about this seems very familiar. I can't quite put my finger on it. Come on, let's regroup."

They both dropped down to join the rest of the team, and, just like that, they were all right back where they started.

"Just relax, everyone," said Brody in a calming voice. "This is all part of the adventure. Go into your backpacks. You'll find some ski goggles. Put them on."

But the goggles only made it easier to see that Felix might have made the right decision by leaving. The snow was pouring down, making every move more treacherous.

"I don't think we can do this," said Jaylan. "It's too dangerous. I wanna go home."

BOOM!

"He's actually got a point," added Alec. "This stuff is falling harder and harder."

BOOM! BOOM!

"Yeah, this is insane," added Bonita. "We're still pretty close to home. Let's go get some hot chocolate."

BOOM! BOOM! BOOM!

Punching Crab looked on, hoping with all his heart

that they wouldn't quit. Felonious looked on, knowing from experience that they probably would.

"So you just want to give up?" yelled Brody. "Stop trying? Already?"

Jaylan simply turned and said, "I prefer to think of it as self-preservation," which meant Jaylan was so worried about his safety that he slid over to the trail and left. It only took a few steps before he was completely out of sight—swallowed by the heavy thundersnow.

Fierce and Fearless

Felonious said nothing. When you are already disappointed in children, you only have so much cynicism in you, which means Felonious didn't have the energy for another lecture. Instead, he just looked at Brody, who now felt the same disappointment. It was obvious. His team wasn't going to fight. They hadn't followed Jaylan yet, but they would soon enough. He could see it in their eyes.

But that's when Jake saw something else. He poked at Brody, who then saw it too. It was Halil. He was doing what kids who have strong connections to their spirit animals do. After all, this was snow. Not concrete. And for Halil, that meant it was time to play. The harder the snow came down, the more Halil seemed to like it. The bigger the flakes, the bigger his smile. And when it started to sleet—a common effect of thundersnow—he actually opened his mouth as if he were drinking from the sky.

Brody got that feeling again. Jake reached into his favorite pants, pulled out a magic rock, and placed it in Brody's palm. Brody squeezed tight.

Trust your instincts.

It was the voice. And Brody listened. When he did, things instantly froze. His body got warm. He took a deep breath, and a few seconds later, everything moved in super slow motion. There was a sharp burst of light and then nothing. It was silent, except for the sound of a beating heart.

THUMP, thump, thump, thump. THUMP, thump, thump, thump.

The beat seemed to be coming from two places: in Brody's own chest and directly in front of him.

THUMP, thump, thump, thump. THUMP, thump, thump, thump. The beats were synchronized. Rhythmical. Perfect.

When Brody looked up, Halil was gone. In his place

was a furry, brown creature with huge paws like snow-shoes. It was running at full speed to stay on top of the snow. That's what this kind of animal does. Brody focused hard. He could see two pale stripes down the animal's back. It kept running. It didn't want to stop. And it didn't. Until it heard this:

"You're a wolverine."

The rest of The Mutiny looked on through their goggles. As for The Eliminators, their jaws dropped to the ground. Uncle Skeeta flashed a simple grin and said quietly, "Perfect."

"Are you dudes seeing what I'm seeing?" Geovanny asked. "How can this be?"

"I don't know," said Brian. "But it's the coolest thing I've ever seen."

"That looks like fun," added Lainey.

"Shh," ordered Rudy.

It seemed as if Brody were floating, moving closer and closer to the wolverine that was Halil. Finally he stopped.

"Your spirit animal," said Brody, staring straight into Halil's eyes. "I saw it. You're a wolverine."

The animal dropped down in the snow. The rest of the

kids circled around him. Suddenly he looked like Halil again.

"I am?" he said. "I'm a wolverine?" It took a second to sink in, but he knew it. For the first time in his life, he felt connected, and it felt good. It felt right in his soul. "I am," he repeated, and this time it wasn't a question. "I am a wolverine."

Then he stood up, and looked around, staring each person right in the eye. And all the kids were staring back. He followed their eyes and felt something around his neck. It was a leather cord. On the end of the leather cord was a magic rock with an imprint of a claw—the claw of a wolverine. Halil held it tight. Then he looked back up at his team.

"And wolverines don't give up," he said. "We are fierce and fearless. So I'm asking you: Are we giving up?"

"No!" yelled Brian, engulfed in the moment.

The Mutiny agreed. And as their cheers echoed louder than the boom from the thundersnow, Brody pulled Jake aside and whispered, "Did that really just happen?"

"You connected him," said Jake. "You connected him to his spirit animal. Just like you did for me."

Brody turned to Punching Crab and the Fish Doctor, who, true to Grammy's agreement, provided no further explanation. But Felonious did nod back, as if to say there was still hope. And Halil proved it when he turned directly into the wind, let out a loud growl, and started to move slowly and steadily right up the mountain that was impossible to climb. He motioned for the team to follow close behind. They stepped where he stepped. They grabbed what he grabbed. He protected them from the elements using his body as a shield, and, step by step, The Mutiny slowly made it to the top.

At Rudy's party, the light on the wall shifted from red to yellow as The Mutiny advanced to Stage 2 in its pursuit of the Illumination at the Sequestered Spring. But the clock was still running: 2 hours, 11 minutes, and 17, 16, 15, 14, 13.

The Armpit

Rudy was right—the snow did make navigating the trails much more challenging. With each step The Mutiny took, they sank deeper and deeper into the snow—first to their shins, then to their knees, then to their thighs. But somehow, the Mutiny stayed on track, and nobody complained. They were too focused on what had just happened.

"Can you do that for me?" Bonita begged, as she and Brody slid across a fallen tree. "Come on, what's my spirit animal?"

"That's not the way it works," said Brody. "I can't control when it happens. It just does."

"Come on," said Bonita. "Just do it for me. What am I?

A Bengal tiger? A dolphin? A wild boar?"

"Why does everyone always assume their spirit animal is a fierce or mighty animal?" wondered Alec.

"Yeah," added Ranjeta. "Why isn't anyone ever a gnat or mosquito?"

The debate over the lamest spirit animal, which ranged from the notoriously lazy sloth to the hideous blobfish, made trudging through the snow seem to go quicker.

"We're gonna do it," sang Brody, expressing the mood of the entire team. "We're gonna do it." And even Punching Crab sang along. But Brody was singing a different tune after Jake gave him a subtle but solid shoulder to the chest.

"Oww!" cried Brody. "What was that for?"

"You always do this," warned Jake. "You get cocky. Stop the singing and stay humble. Stay focused. We still have a long way to go."

"You know what you always do? You worry too much," countered Brody. "My middle name is humble. I mean no one is humbler than I am. I'm the best, most humblest person in the Whoaaaaaaaaa."

In case you've never fallen 15 feet into a big, long pit, that's the sound you'd probably make.

"Got 'em," said Rudy, as he watched one member of The Mutiny after another slide into the hole. The Eliminators had chosen among more than 257 traps and decided to create the Armpit, because falling into a dark, deep pit was only the beginning.

"What's that?" asked Bonita, sticking her nose in the air and sniffing.

"You mean that nasty, disgusting stink that smells like some big, fat ogre has us in a headlock?" asked Halil, holding his nose, which, unfortunately, could smell just a little better than before, thanks to his new spirit animal.

"Actually," said Bonita. "I was talking about the thing that just grabbed me."

Brody reached into his backpack and pulled out a flashlight, which promptly fell to the ground when his arm was seized as well.

"What's in here?" cried Bonita.

The flashlight revealed a bunch of arms reaching out from the dirt.

"This pit is filled with starfish," explained Brody, adding that some starfish actually have as many as 40 arms. "And the really cool part," he continued, "is that if a starfish is threatened by a predator, it can drop an arm, get away, and grow a new one."

"How is that going to help us?" asked Ranjeta. "We're the ones being threatened here."

There was a combination of pride and delight as Rudy and the rest of his team watched their rivals struggle to move, let alone escape the clutches of the Armpit.

Brody, who was too strong to be held down, and Jake, who was too quick, struggled to free their friends from the arms of the starfish, but they didn't call it the Armpit for nothing: each time Brody or Jake pulled one arm away, another took its place.

"We're not going to make it," said Bonita.

"I can't breathe," cried Ranjeta, as dirt started falling in from the sides of the pit.

"Stay calm," growled Halil, but there was nothing he could do either.

There was really only one thing to do, and Alec was doing it. After all, this was a big hole of dirt. And for kids who have strong connections to their spirit animals, dirt is meant for digging. The more dirt that came down, the harder Alec dug. Even with one arm snagged by a starfish arm, the other arm could still dig. When Jake helped him free both arms, he pulled off his gloves so the dirt could collect under his fingernails. That's fun.

As he watched Alec dig and dig, Brody smiled and looked at Jake, who reached into his pocket and pulled out another rock.

Trust your instincts, the voice in Brody's head said.

And when Brody did, things instantly froze. Brody's body got as warm as the wires. He took a deep breath, and a few seconds later, everything moved in super slow motion. There was a sharp burst of light, and then nothing. It was silent, except for the sound of a beating heart.

THUMP, thump, thump, thump. THUMP, thump, thump, thump.

When Brody looked, Alec was gone. In his place was a gray, furry mammal, with a broad build, muscular back, and terrific claws. It was digging at top speed and actually creating more space and air with its effort. That's what these kinds of animals do. It didn't want to stop. And it didn't. Until it heard this:

"You're a badger," said Brody, staring straight into the eyes of the creature. "Your spirit animal. You're a badger."

Alec dropped down for just a second, and the rest of the team cleared the dirt away so he could breathe. Suddenly he looked like Alec again. It took a second to sink in, but he knew it. For the first time in his life, he felt connected, and it felt good. It felt right in his soul. "I am," he repeated with certainty. "I'm a badger."

There was little time to celebrate, so Alec didn't hesitate. He popped to his feet and looked down around his neck. The leather cord was just like Jake's, Brody's, and Halil's, but the imprint on the rock was different. It was a long, sharp tooth. The tooth of the badger.

"We badgers protect ourselves and our friends at all costs," said Alec. "Follow me."

Then, with the amazing digging ability that allows badgers to easily catch other underground rodents, combined with the ferocity that helps them earn their reputation as one of the most fearless animals, Alec starting digging upward. Faster and faster he went, creating what turned into an underground escalator that led the entire team, and several starfish, up to safety.

"That looked pretty cool," said Jared.

What was also cool or not, depending on which

team you were rooting for, was when the light switched from yellow to green, signifying that The Mutiny had now reached Stage 3.

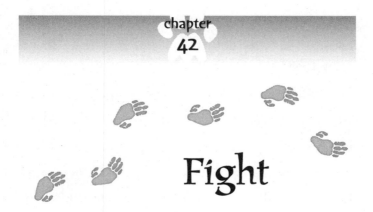

Fight

Breath shot from Jake's mouth like the fire from a dragon as he stormed over to Brody and pulled him away from the rest of the group. Not even The Eliminators could hear what they were talking about, but it didn't take long before they all understood he wasn't asking for the recipe for Brody's famous stuffed French toast. Jake pointed two fingers to his eyes, then to Brody, and sternly said, "You're going down."

"Where did this come from?" asked Kai, watching with surprise. "What could they be fighting about?"

"You don't understand these guys," explained Rudy, who'd been around enough to know that arguments between Jake and Brody could start faster than a peregrine falcon flies. "They don't need a reason to fight. They're brothers."

"You're supposed to be the leader of this group," yelled Jake, right on cue. "But you only think of yourself." He punctuated his point with a firm push in the shoulder.

"You just like to blame other people for your problems," responded Brody, who added a little push of his own. "That's why your soul is so dark."

That line made Rudy smile because he knew what was coming next. Without any warning, Jake tackled Brody and pushed his face in the snow. Brody rolled away and tripped Jake with a leg whip. Halil, Alec, and Ranjeta tried to break it up, but they couldn't. Bonita was always up for a good fight, so she just sat back and enjoyed it. Felonious and Punching Crab agreed they couldn't get involved even if they wanted to.

"If you're so powerful, how come you didn't know that pit was coming?" Jake yelled. "What are all those instincts for if you can't even use them?"

He pushed Brody in the chest, causing him to take a couple steps back.

"I'll show you how powerful I am," countered Brody. "I'm not letting you beat me up anymore. I'm going to stick up for myself. I'm getting bigger and stronger."

"The only thing getting bigger is your ego. Maybe if you would start using it and stop thinking you're so great all the time, we wouldn't get stuck in all these traps."

"Yeah, well, if it weren't for me, you'd never even have your spirit animal," said Brody. "Maybe if I didn't have to spend so much time helping you, I could focus on my surroundings."

"You couldn't focus if you were a camera," said Jake.

"You couldn't focus if you were a girl scout," Brody responded.

"That doesn't even make any sense."

"Well you don't make any sense," replied Brody. "You never make sense. You never do anything. And now you're trying to take over even though you're the one that's killing us out here."

"You got one part of that right," said Jake. "I'm going to kill you."

He rushed over and put Brody in a headlock. But Brody was definitely getting bigger and stronger, and he quickly broke free. Back and forth it went, until Brody took a running start, and with the force of a charging bull, he lunged right into the shoulder Jake had bruised only a week ago.

Jake didn't yell. He didn't say a word. He just held his arm and stared straight ahead. Part of Brody wanted to go over to see if Jake was okay. The other part wanted to stand tall, as if to say, "You mess with the bull, you get the horns." Brody settled on something in the middle. Just standing straight, his hands at his side, waiting to see how Jake would react. For a short moment, they both just stood a few feet apart staring at each other.

Finally, Jake walked over and handed Brody the remaining rocks. "You think you're so tough," he said. "Go ahead and do this on your own. I'm outta here."

"That's perfect," Brody yelled as Jake started walking away, his right arm braced gingerly across his stomach. "Go ahead and leave. You never really cared about any of this anyway. You never believed in anything. That's why we'll be better off without you."

Both teams watched in shock as Jake just kept walking, turned down a distant path, and vanished out of sight.

"And then there were five," said Rudy, who always loved to see Jake and Brody battle. And he especially loved it when he looked up at the board and saw the light that read *Jake* go dark.

The Distractiplier

Brody Boondoggle moved slowly at first—trying to ignore thoughts of his brother and how his separate journey was going. But then he realized time was the enemy now, so he picked up the pace, jumping over logs, ducking under branches, and sliding down hills as he led his team through the final twists and turns that he knew would lead directly to the Sequestered Spring.

"How are those dudes doing this?" yelled Geovanny. "They survived the thundersnow. They survived the Armpit. It doesn't make sense. They don't even have a control panel."

"I have to say, it looks like a pretty cool adventure," acknowledged Brian.

Rudy ignored that comment and instead concentrated his attention on the path he assumed Brody would need to follow to reach his final destination.

"I got it," said Rudy. "These guys proved they're pretty strong. Now let's see how smart they are."

The pink and green wires grew warm, although not as warm since Cole and Lainey had lost a little interest and Jared was only going through the motions. But Rudy was strong, and Geovanny was willing, which gave them plenty of energy to put their next idea into action.

Suddenly The Mutiny wasn't heading for one path anymore; they were heading for seven. "That's the multiplier," declared Rudy. But that wasn't all. Everything about these paths was enticing, meaning each one seemed like the perfect way to go. "And that's the distraction," he added.

"It's the Distractiplier," proclaimed Geovanny. "Just what we needed."

All eyes turned to Brody as if he would know what to do. But even after looking with his third eye, calling on all his instincts, and trusting his elite spirit-animal skills, he didn't. "They all look, smell, and sound exactly the same," observed Brody.

"Oh, this is great, just great," cried Bonita. "We'll never have time to check them all out," she added, hiking a few steps down the first path before retreating.

"The problem is they all seem so good," said Halil.

"We could just pick one and hope for the best," suggested Alec. "But I don't like our chances." And even though Brody didn't want to admit it, he didn't like them either.

That was until he looked up and saw Ranjeta. She wasn't kicking the snow in disgust like Bonita or punching the air in frustration like Halil or continually throwing herself headfirst into a snowbank for some unknown reason, like Alec. She was calmly investigating her surroundings, like a kid with a strong connection to her spirit animal. After all, figuring out what to do when one path turns into seven is kind of like a puzzle. And solving puzzles is fun.

Brody grabbed a rock from his pocket. When he did, things instantly froze. His body got warm again, and a few seconds later, everything moved in super slow motion. There was a sharp burst of light, and then, well, you know the rest.

THUMP, thump, thump, thump. THUMP, thump, thump, thump.

The next thing he knew, Ranjeta was gone. In her place was a sea creature with three hearts and eight arms. The arms were covered in suction cups and attached to a body with no internal skeleton, meaning it was so soft it could easily squeeze through very tiny spaces.

"You're an octopus," stated Brody. "Your spirit animal. It's an octopus."

The creature, which many people are surprised to learn is considered perhaps the most intelligent of all invertebrates, looked up. Brody focused back on the octopus. It was Ranjeta again, only with a leather cord hanging from her neck. On the leather cord was a rock, and on the rock was an imprint of a tentacle. That's when the octopus inside Ranjeta took control.

"We octopuses know how to avoid trouble," said Ranjeta proudly. "So let's think about this." She walked over to the first path and then continued moving from path to path. They all seemed so right, and that's what made Ranjeta think something might be wrong. She continued to shake her head back and forth as she inspected each one.

"Well," said Halil. "Which path do we take?"

Ranjeta thought for a second. Then she looked up and

announced, "None of them."

"What?" said Alec.

"What?" repeated Rudy.

"What . . . else do we have to eat around here?" said Brian, who was only partially paying attention to the game.

"You heard me," said Ranjeta. "I know how to spot a trap. And that's exactly what this feels like to me."

"But the right path has to be somewhere," said Alec.

Ranjeta rotated around, and that's when she noticed an old, decaying ceramic pipe sticking out of the riverbank, directly opposite the middle path. The entry to the pipe was no bigger than the size of a large pizza and was covered in a thick sheet of ice, except for a small hole in the bottom, where water continually dripped into the river below.

She pointed her finger to the pipe and announced, "We're going that way."

"Why?" asked Bonita.

"Because when everyone is expecting you to do one thing," explained Ranjeta, "sometimes it's best to do something else."

"But how are we going to get in?" asked Alec, banging

on the ice that covered the entry. "This ice is too thick to break."

Ranjeta thought for a second. Then she traced her steps back to the center path, dropped to her hands, and quickly started clearing away the snow. She motioned for Alec, Halil, and Bonita to help, and now there were eight arms, just like an octopus, working furiously to solve the puzzle.

"What are we looking for?" asked Alec.

Ranjeta looked over to Brody. "It's your dream," she said. "It's got to be around here somewhere."

A few seconds later, she cleared away enough snow to reveal a long, narrow hole in the ground. "I knew it," she said.

"How?" asked Halil, and everyone was wondering the same thing.

"I just did," answered Ranjeta, winking at Brody.

Ranjeta reached into her backpack and pulled out a flashlight. She shined the light into the deep hole and peered down. "I double knew it," she said. "There's something down there. It looks like a crystal or something. But it's definitely the key we're looking for."

Without wasting a second, Alec pushed Ranjeta aside

and started digging as fast as any badger could—but the ground didn't budge. Halil tried to force his arm down as far as he could—but wolverines don't have arms as long as telephone poles. Bonita attempted to thread a long stick deep into the hole—but that didn't work either.

Brody concentrated on an elephant's trunk, a giraffe's neck, even a long-tailed grass lizard, for obvious reasons, but he continually came up just short, just like in his dream.

"None of our physical gifts will help us now," said Ranjeta, explaining what Punching Crab and Felonious Fish already knew. "We have to use our brains."

Ranjeta thought for a second. How could they get the crystal up from the bottom of the hole if they couldn't reach it, dig for it, or fish it out with a stick?

"Come on," she said, "there's always an answer." She looked back at the pipe, the rhythmic sounds of the water dripping out and hitting the rocks below like a drum. It was trying to talk to her. And then she finally heard.

"What are you doing?" asked Halil, as Ranjeta grabbed her water bottle, opened the top, and poured all the water straight down the hole. She didn't answer. She just grabbed

Halil's water bottle and poured the water down the hole as well. She did the same with Alec's water bottle and Bonita's and Brody's too.

"That dudette's gone mad," said Geovanny. "She's wasting all their water."

"I don't think so," figured Jared. "She's using it to make whatever is in that hole float to the top."

"Pretty smart," acknowledged Brian, while chomping on a corn dog.

When the last water bottle was empty, Ranjeta directed her friends to stand evenly along the route from the pipe to the hole. Bonita quickly filled a bottle with water from the pipe and threw it to Alec, who tossed it to Halil, who chucked it to Brody, who lobbed it to Ranjeta, who poured it into the hole. They did it over and over, like a finely tuned machine until. . . ."I got it," announced Ranjeta, scooping a long crystal-like icicle out of the hole and sprinting directly toward the pipe.

Without breaking stride, she jabbed the icicle into the hole at the bottom of the pipe as hard as she could. It was like a mini explosion. The cover of the pipe shattered, revealing a long dark tunnel. Brody glanced over at

Ranjeta, who nodded, and everyone immediately understood. They all took a few steps back and then, just like octopuses, squeezed through the hole. After the first few feet, the tunnel widened, and everyone plummeted straight down and out of sight.

While Rudy was experiencing utter frustration as orange lights blinked over and over, signifying that Stage 4 had been reached, Brody and his team were experiencing total perfection—cruising down the waterslide from his dream. And when it finally ended, the game was over. They were at the Sequestered Spring.

All Heart

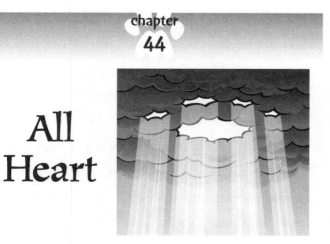

Absolute brilliance radiated from the Sequestered Spring; but that's not what made Brody feel so right. A collection of tall and powerful trees protected the area from the ice and snow, creating a warm, comfortable climate; but that's not what made Brody feel so safe. And while the walk down the path that led to the very heart of the Sequestered Spring was lined with incredibly exotic and beautiful flowers, that's not what made Brody Boondoggle feel as if he were finally home.

Thump, thump, thump, thump.

It was that beat. It was coming from the very center of his heart.

Thump, thump, thump, thump. Thump, thump, thump, thump.

Brody could hear it. It was beating, stronger and stronger, and it was at that point that he truly understood anything was possible.

"We did it," Brody whispered to himself, fighting the urge to be cocky. Even Felonious was lost in the awe of the moment. "It's more beautiful than I ever imagined," he said to Punching Crab. "They really did it."

But not really. Not yet.

"So what do we do now?" asked Ranjeta, as if to remind everyone that the overall mission was still far from over.

Brody was thinking the same thing. But although he'd never seen anything like it, it all seemed very familiar. He pointed to four of the trees—trees not as tall as the dozens of trees that surrounded that area, but that marked the corners of a perfect square with four equal sides. The grass directly in the center of the square had been trimmed or cut—or something that perhaps we can't even understand—in a way that left a paw print. All eyes fixed on Brody as he started walking. It seemed more like floating, but even though he was now 12 years old, he still couldn't float. But ask everyone there, and they'll swear he was floating right to the center of that square.

Once there, Brody inspected the paw print, which was like nothing that he could identify. But it looked exactly like the paw print hanging around his neck.

Best birthday present ever, he thought to himself.

Instinctively, Brody lifted his necklace over his head and placed it perfectly into the matching print on the ground. There was a soft click, which seemed to signal to the clouds that it was now time to move out of the way, but only just enough to create a hole that was the exact shape of the paw print.

Brody smiled. He knew this was the moment of the Illumination, and so did his friends. After all they'd been through, they had finally made it. Everything felt so right. They were at the right spot at the right moment in time.

A dense light emerged from the clouds above and slowly descended upon Brody. If the legend was correct, a sharp burst of light would shine through the hole in the clouds, ricochet off Brody's necklace, and open the portal to Sarraka. It would remain open for six minutes. The Akaway would be saved. There would once again be balance in the universe.

Brody stayed perfectly still, staring straight ahead. The time was getting closer and closer. Brody was ready. It would only be another instant. Nothing could stop him now. He had won. Or at least that's what he thought until he heard a noise so deafening that he truly believed his head would explode.

chapter
45

Emergency Wipeout

Brody Boondoggle wasn't supposed to get this far, but neither was Uncle Skeeta, whose entire life was filled with people who would tell him what he couldn't do instead of showing him what was possible. But that's a story for a different book. The point is that, with some help from Grammy, Uncle Skeeta had proved them all wrong. In his mind, he was the most powerful person in the world—after all, if you control the children, you control the future—so even though he never dreamed Brody Boondoggle would figure out a way to overcome all those obstacles and defeat his latest game in time to be standing in the most magical and sacred place in the universe, he had a plan, just in case

Brody did.

It was called the Emergency Wipeout, and he programmed it into the video game just for this reason. If activated, it would basically create a concentrated supersonic wave of noise so loud and so intense that it would temporarily paralyze any man, woman, or child in its path. Just imagine what it would do to someone with the heightened senses of an Akaway.

The plan was perfect. It was smart. It was thorough, it was. . . .

"Not fair," said Rudy after Uncle Skeeta summoned him to the control room and explained the concept behind the Emergency Wipeout. "It could really hurt him, and I don't think it's right."

"It's just a game," said Uncle Skeeta. "It's not even real." But one look in Rudy's dark brown eyes, and Uncle Skeeta knew that Rudy knew that it was very real indeed.

"Okay," conceded Uncle Skeeta. "But *hurting* is such a strong word. I like to think of it as *disabling*, only temporarily."

"But it was just supposed to be a game," said Rudy. "And this just seems wrong."

"And I respect that," said Uncle Skeeta. "But let me ask you this: Do you think he cares about you?" Uncle Skeeta paused. "If your friend had a choice to make, do you think he would choose you? You have special powers, too, you know. You're as strong as he is, maybe stronger someday, if you stick with me. And I know you, Rudy. Losing to Brody doesn't feel good. Does it?"

Rudy didn't answer, which Uncle Skeeta rightfully took as a no.

"I didn't think so," he continued. "So the question is: Are you with me or against me?"

"With you or against you?" questioned Rudy. "What does that even mean?"

"It means this," said Uncle Skeeta. "I need a partner. A very special partner who I can count on. Who will help me move above and beyond what we're doing now. We can do magical things that most people can't even imagine. That's what this is all about. It's about capturing the future. Our future. Your future."

It all made perfect sense to Rudy. So when Uncle Skeeta asked, "Is that a future you think you'd like?" Rudy said, "Yes."

"Well then, you have to take control of your future," continued Uncle Skeeta. "Choose your path. You started this when you told me where to find the last Akaway. I didn't ask you to do it, you just did. It's who you are. Well, that was the beginning. Now it's time to finish it."

chapter 46

The Opposite of Fun

It began as a murmur on the ground, like an earthquake. Then it started to rise, like toxic gas escaping from under a door. At first, petals started falling off the flowers, and then the entire garden just wilted, as if life were slowly being sucked away. The vibrations climbed higher and higher, starting at Brody's feet, then moving to his shins, to his knees, and engulfing him as if he were trapped in a bathtub slowly filling with water.

He had no idea what it was, but he could feel it climb up his thighs, through his waist, past his shoulders to his head, which felt as if it were caught in a vise, and someone was slowly and steadily turning, squeezing the power right out of him.

"This should end it once and for all," said Rudy, who now fully embraced his new path, just as Uncle Skeeta knew he would. Rudy had returned to be with the rest of his team, explained the situation to them, and lied, reinforcing the idea that they were just playing a video game.

"But it seems so real," said Cole.

The room was quiet. They watched as Brody tried to fight the force with all his might—many of the kids on The Eliminators were secretly rooting for Brody—but it was no use. The power was too strong, even for a kid with the power of an Akaway, especially for a kid with the power of an Akaway. Brody fell to the ground, his arms covering his ears as he rolled in agony.

"We have to help him," said Ranjeta, who sprinted into the circle, only to be knocked back by the force of the vibrations. Halil, Alec, and Bonita helped her up, and now all four fought their way forward. But even with all the fight and ferocity their spirit animals could provide, it was like walking against the winds of a hurricane, and with each small step towards Brody, the pain in their heads became more and more intense.

"Nooooo," Brody yelled in a loud, booming, terrifying roar. "Get up," he motioned. "Get up."

"We're not going to leave you here," said Bonita.

"You can't help me," Brody said. "Help yourself. Get up into the trees."

Brody was right. They couldn't help him now. Nobody could. So up, up, up, away from the vibrations they climbed, which only gave them a better view of Brody's demise, meaning his eyes were vibrating, his body was pulsating, and his head felt like a water balloon just about to pop.

"Come on now," said Jared. "I don't want it to end like this. Even if this is just a game."

"Yeah," added Brian. "What kind of party is this anyway? I thought it was going to be fun. Well, this isn't fun."

"I agree," added Cole. "That's enough."

"Mutiny, Mutiny," chanted The Eliminators. But to Rudy, those were just the cries of weak children who had no idea what was truly at stake. He was his uncle's nephew, now more than ever, so he calmly turned around, removed his helmet, and with a golden smile announced, "The party's over. Thank you so much for coming."

One by one, The Eliminators pulled off their helmets, unclipped their harnesses, and walked away. Rudy continued to watch the screen as the grooves in the grass that Brody used to summon the Illumination were being destroyed, causing the ray from the sky to reverse. The force from the Emergency Wipeout then shattered Brody's necklace.

That rock is in a thousand pieces right now, thought Rudy. His smile betrayed the last remaining piece of compassion that was fighting deep inside for survival. *There's nothing he can do now*, he thought. *Absolutely nothing.*

Analyzing Spitball

And then it stopped.

The vibrations. The pounding. Even the monitor on which Rudy and Uncle Skeeta were watching. All just magically turned off. Just like that.

Well, maybe not magically. There may have been a reasonable explanation, and Rudy and Uncle Skeeta went running out of the game room to check on it. They rushed up the stairs, took a left, and darted down the long hallway to the room with the green glow under the door. But this time, there was no glow, and in that moment, Uncle Skeeta knew exactly what had happened.

Rudy, on the other hand, had no idea, and when he

opened the door to the server that controlled the entire video game system, his eyes widened, his jaw dropped, and his face became as white as if he had seen a ghost.

But it wasn't a ghost at all. Just someone who had been off Rudy's radar since Stage 3. And if he hadn't been so focused on Brody's doom, he might have felt the spirit of an ocelot sneak into the house and eavesdrop on his conversation with Uncle Skeeta about the Emergency Wipeout. He might have seen this same spirit animal sneak upstairs to the room that Uncle Skeeta dared him to enter only a few days earlier and challenge the pig who was guarding the door by pointing two fingers to his eyes, then at the pig, and saying, "You're going down once and for all."

And he might have heard the fight that ensued. The one with the punching and wrestling and squealing. The one in which one creature was fighting for his job, but the other one was fighting for his brother. And when you combine a righteous mission with a spirit animal who will fight to its death, there's no chance you're going to lose to a pig named Gizmo.

Of course, the door to the room was still protected by the most powerful lock ever made. The one with the bars made out of an indestructible metal alloy. The one that could only be unlocked by Uncle Skeeta, or at least by his saliva.

But Grammy had taken care of that during her meeting with him. It would have been nice for Uncle Skeeta to stay out of the adventure, but Grammy knew him better than that. The important part of that agreement was Uncle Skeeta's spit that was used to seal the deal. That saliva went from his hand to Grammy's—if you watched closely, you saw that Grammy only pretended to spit so Uncle Skeeta's saliva would stay pure. Uncle Skeeta didn't know it, but his pure saliva then went from Grammy's hand to a small, glass container, which preserved the spit long enough for Grammy to get it home intact and turn it into the perfect spitball.

From there, the perfect spitball went into a straw that was given to Jake as a present, even though it was Brody's birthday. Jake had one shot and one shot only after locking Gizmo in the closet down the hall. He took the straw and the spitball from the long white box in the inside pocket of his winter coat, aimed it at the target on the lock's entry chamber, and fired.

"Analyzing spitball," said the robotic voice that came from the speaker on the door after Jake hit the heart of the target. Seconds later, the same voice said, "Hello, Uncle Skeeta. You are looking good today. The bald head is working for you." The bars on the door slid open, and that's when Jake walked in and pulled the plug on all Uncle Skeeta's dreams.

So there they were—Jake holding the plug, and Uncle Skeeta holding the door.

"Sorry I didn't RSVP earlier," said Jake, breathing heavily. "Hope I'm not too late for the party."

"Oh, but you are," said Uncle Skeeta, whose sweaty forehead made him appear just a little more frazzled than before. "That was excellent work, though. I gotta give you guys credit. Getting through this door was pretty impressive."

"No better way to know someone than to infiltrate their surroundings," said Jake.

"Apparently not," agreed Uncle Skeeta. "And faking that fight with your brother. Pretty impressive."

"Yeah, faking, right," said Jake. "Thanks. I really owe that to you as well. Or at least to your video games. If they weren't so good, I wouldn't have played so many over the years, and then I wouldn't have recognized your work during the hike. But there was just no mistaking it."

"I'm flattered," said Uncle Skeeta. "But there's just one problem. None of this matters. We already blocked the Illumination, the Akaway will be no more, and there's really nothing you or your brother can do about it." He took a few steps toward Jake. "You don't get it. There's nothing that can happen that I'm not prepared for, that won't benefit me. I've worked too hard to leave anything to chance."

"I don't know what that means," said Jake. "But I'm not waiting around to find out."

Jake stormed for the door and, in that moment, made a mental note never to play a game of Red Rover with a bum shoulder, because when he tried to break through the wall made by Uncle Skeeta and Rudy, he bounced right off them and landed flat on the floor.

Suddenly, a strong hand came down and helped Jake to his feet. "No need to run, little man," said Uncle Skeeta. "I'm taking you with me."

The Most Noble Reason of All

Whether you were looking up from the ground like Brody Boondoggle, or down from way up in the trees, like his friends, one thing was clear: The imprint that triggered the Illumination was gone, just like Brody's necklace. So even though the pain in Brody's head was now gone as well, it had shifted to his heart, because he knew that, without the imprint and without his necklace, there was no way to open the portal, save the Akaway, and bring balance to the universe.

"You can come down now," Brody yelled to his friends. "It's over. There's nothing more we can do."

But his friends didn't agree. Because the truth is that

when you have just learned that you have the special powers of a wolverine or a badger or an octopus, there's always more you can do—even if it's just continuing to climb maybe the greatest climbing trees this world has ever seen. And that's what Ranjeta, Halil, and Alec did. Even Bonita, for the moment forgetting that she desperately wanted to learn her spirit animal, kept climbing.

And here's the best part. They didn't do it to avoid the bad guys or escape the sonic vibrations or even to score points in a video game. They did it for the most noble reason of all: Climbing trees is fun. And, sometimes, that's just the kind of magic you need to bring balance back to the universe.

And that's exactly what happened.

Ranjeta discovered it first. For an octopus, she was quite a climber. In fact, she didn't stop climbing until she reached the very top of the tallest tree. That's where she saw it. It looked strange at first—the imprint in the tree—but when she tilted her head to the left and then to the right for a different perspective, it started to seem familiar. Finally, she peered down, and she knew. The design in the tree was the exact same as the one on her necklace.

She removed her necklace and matched the print to the one in the tree. She pressed gently. There was a soft click.

"Brody," she yelled. "It's not over. It's not over."

"What are you talking about?" he screamed. He was lying on his back, marveling at the cloud that looked like a rabbit eating an ice cream cone.

"I'm talking about the imprint," Ranjeta yelled back.

"I know," replied Brody. "It's gone."

"No, it's not. There's one up in this tree. And it's a perfect match."

"A perfect match for what?"

"For the print on my spirit-animal necklace."

Brody sprang to his feet. And he must have regained most of his power because he could see Ranjeta's necklace resting perfectly in the tree. But still nothing was happening. He turned his head quickly.

"Halil," Brody yelled. Halil was lying comfortably on a branch, checking out the cloud that looked like a water buffalo playing the harmonica. "Can you climb to the top?"

Halil climbed higher and higher until he finally reached the top branch. And there, he saw it too. Right on the trunk of the tree—an impression that fit the one on his necklace perfectly.

Click.

There were two more trees. Alec was deep into a game of hide-and-seek with a salamander when he heard Brody's call. A short, skillful climb later, and he, too, was at the top of his tree, staring straight at an imprint that perfectly matched the one around his neck.

Click.

Just one more to go, and Bonita knew it as tears started to form in her eyes. She was next, but there was nothing she could do. Brody hadn't connected her.

"Just climb," Brody yelled.

So Bonita did. She climbed as fast as she could. Brody tried, but he saw nothing. The last rock, he remembered, and reached into his pocket. But it was gone as well. Bonita reached the top of the tree and looked down.

Brody just shook his head. An eerie calm engulfed Bonita as she thought about all she had accomplished today. Surviving the snow, breaking free of the Armpit, solving the Distractiplier, climbing the tree.

That's when she heard a sound.

"Thump, thump, thump, thump." And that's when she

realized that Brody would never connect her to her spirit animal.

Trust your instincts, said her little voice. *You're already connected.*

She looked to the ground and saw Punching Crab. He smiled. She looked down around her neck and saw a leather cord holding the final magic rock.

You're a tiger shark, said the voice, and the animal that was both strong and many times misunderstood felt right to Bonita. And when she looked straight ahead, the print in the rock matched the one in the tree perfectly.

Click.

chapter
49

The Quad

The vibrations started again from the ground. But the aura did not indicate pain as it had before. This aura contained a sea of positive energy that signified life. Brody looked up. The clouds started to form again, just as Uncle Skeeta, Rudy, and Jake raced in. So respectful of the Sequestered Spring was Uncle Skeeta that he parked his snowmobile a safe distance away so that the exhaust didn't upset the harmony of the area.

"They've discovered the quad," said Uncle Skeeta.

"No. Not the quad! Not the quad!" screamed Rudy. Then he paused. "What's the quad?"

Uncle Skeeta pointed to the four trees and then to the clouds. It was at that moment that a tiny, pin-like hole was starting to form. From that hole shot a concentrated, sharp beam of light aimed directly at Brody. The power of the ray intensified, meaning it was pushing down on Brody harder and harder.

"You need to use your spirit-animal necklace to reflect the ray back into the sky," yelled Jake.

"It's a little difficult seeing how it was shattered into a thousand pieces," replied Brody.

"Look around," yelled Jake. "Maybe there's something else you can use."

"I'm a little busy right now," said Brody. "Maybe that's something you could do."

While Jake searched furiously for a piece of glass, a mirror, or anything that could return the beam back to the sky, Brody focused all his energy on being a locust because they have leg muscles that, for their size, are more than a thousand times stronger than a human's. But a beam that is strong enough to open a portal to a different world is certainly more powerful than a locust, even a human-sized one, so even though Brody was stronger now than ever before, his legs still started to weaken, until he finally dropped to his knees.

"It's draining all of his powers," Uncle Skeeta said, trying to educate Rudy as much as possible. "If he doesn't get out of there, he'll lose his spirit animal forever."

"But if he does, he'll have no chance to open the portal," reasoned Rudy.

"That does create an interesting dilemma," concluded Uncle Skeeta.

"Get out of there," yelled Jake, waving his arms. "You've got to protect your spirit animal. You've got to save yourself." Brody felt the bite above the outside corner of his left eye, then he looked over at his big brother, and, in that look, Jake knew what Brody was thinking: This is more important than just one person, and I'm not going anywhere.

It can kill you or it can make you stronger, said Brody's little voice. *There are lots of ways to be strong. And showing courage is one of the best ways of all.*

"Just find me something shiny to reflect this light," Brody yelled. "I can't hang on much longer."

"I don't have anything," said Jake.

He tapped his pockets, front and back. He pulled out his notebook, the one that had provided so many answers but was absolutely useless now. Then he reached into his other back pocket and found something he'd completely forgotten about—the video game with the reflective mirror on the back. The one that was created by the very person he was now working to defeat.

Rudy lunged to stop him, but he was no match for Jake. Grimacing from the pain of his shoulder, Jake chucked the video game as hard as he could right at Brody, who reached up his hand, like the tongue of a toad, and snatched it right out of the air.

I'm an Akaway, he thought to himself.

Suddenly Brody had the power and the equipment to reflect the ray back into the sky. And when that beam shot up into the sky like a rocket, and an equally impressive beam came back down, there was no doubt in anyone's mind that the portal was open, the Akaway was saved, and there was balance in the universe.

The Sarcastic Clap

There is no better weather for celebrating than a steady shower of warm, soft, refreshing rain, and that's exactly what was falling down on Brody and all his friends. Halil, Ranjeta, Bonita, and Alec scurried down from the trees. Jake broke away from Uncle Skeeta and joined the others as they jumped and danced and celebrated as if they had just found the pot of gold at the end of the rainbow or discovered a cure for school or brought balance back to the universe.

Instantly, the rain washed away all the trouble and worry that had weighed so heavily on Brody Boondoggle. Just the sound of rain could do that—cascading against the

leaves, rhythmically pounding the puddles like a drum-
beat until the dirt turns to mud, which naturally causes a
mud fight, which is one of the absolute best ways to have
fun. It wasn't long before Punching Crab's excitement got
the best of him. He sprinted right toward the group, shouted "Dog pile," and threw himself on top of the scrum so
he could celebrate in the mud as well.

Unfortunately, nothing ruins a rain-soaked, mud-
fighting celebration more than somebody performing
a sarcastic clap. You know the one. It starts with just one
clap. There's a long pause. Then another clap and another
long pause. Again and again. Finally, everyone having fun
stops what they're doing and just looks over at the person
clapping and smiling like they're about to share a dirty
little secret, just because they can.

"I have to say, I'm proud of you guys," said Uncle Skeeta.
He was still clapping, but it was slower now and much
softer. He looked to Ranjeta and Bonita, "and ladies."

Now he stopped clapping altogether and just slowly
approached the muddy pack, scooping up some mud of
his own and rubbing it between his fingers. Then he wiped
it on his pants. He looked down, checked his watch, and

then raised his head again.

"Remember I told you there was no way you were going to win. Do you think I mentioned that for my health? Because I was trying to scare you? Because I didn't have anything else to do with my life? No," he continued. "I said it because I believe in being perfectly honest with kids. So here's the dirty little truth: If you didn't open the portal, the Akaway would now be extinct, and we would have won. But that didn't happen." He shrugged. "No worries. Because part of being a genius is making sure you benefit from every situation. And that's what we've done." He paused quickly and checked his watch again. "You see, we had a plan just in case you succeeded. So now that you opened the portal and saved the Akaway, that's going to be even better."

"What are you talking about?" asked Ranjeta.

"I'm talking about what Brody and his brother here already know. That there have been people trying to open that portal for generations. There is amazing power on the other side of that portal for anyone who is smart enough, creative enough, and persistent enough to pursue it."

"What kind of power?" asked Halil.

"That, my friend, we don't know yet," said Uncle Skeeta. "But let's just say it'll make all our dreams come true." But before Uncle Skeeta could go on, there came a question from a trembling voice, meaning Punching Crab was afraid of what the answer to his next question would be. But he asked it anyway.

"Who's we?" he asked, the mud dripping off his shell.

Uncle Skeeta smirked and shook his head, but Jake and Brody didn't give him a chance to answer.

"Felonious," they said together, and all eyes turned toward the fish, who just took his fins, pointed them at Punching Crab as if they were guns, and made two quick clicking sounds with his tongue.

Click, Click.

And with that everyone knew.

"This is becoming a habit," said Uncle Skeeta. "But once again I say congratulations. How'd you know?"

Brody and Jake didn't feel the need to explain. So they didn't say how they first suspected something when Felonious was fishnapped because a fish that smart wouldn't get caught, and, if he did, it wouldn't be by someone who would attempt it in such a clumsy manner. Or that their suspicions were heightened when they heard Uncle Skeeta refer to the Fish Doctor as *Felonious*, a name only a friend would know. Or that they were completely convinced when Felonious used the same phrase as Uncle Skeeta had used to describe the importance of the mission: "This is about making dreams come true."

They didn't say any of that. Instead, Brody just sighed and said, "We just knew."

"Well, I guess I wasn't paying attention," said Punching Crab, tears starting to form in his beady eyes.

"Oh, grow up," Felonious yelled, glaring at Punching Crab. "This is business." He then looked at Brody and Jake, who noticed Felonious checking his watch as well. "And I have both of you to thank," he continued. "It's because of you that I met my new business partner."

"That's right," confirmed Uncle Skeeta. "All I wanted to do was snag the fish so he couldn't tell you about the Sequestered Spring. But that fish is like a ninja. We couldn't catch him. Luckily, he caught us. Then we started talking, and we realized there was a bigger picture. A way to make all our dreams come true. We had a plan all along. First we gave you clues about the fishnapping to test you to see if you were really "the one." Well, you were, no doubt. So then, we decided to help you open the portal."

"Help us?" interrupted Ranjeta. "You did everything you could to stop us."

"That's how we helped you," explained Felonious. "Not just anyone can find the Sequestered Spring, let alone open the portal. I've tried to do it hundreds of times, but I never could. I didn't prove myself against all odds. How could I? I didn't have a righteous motive. But you kids did. You just needed a little help proving it. And, I have to hand it to you—you passed all the tests. You really did it."

If Punching Crab had a jaw, it would have dropped to the ground listening to Felonious admit his plan with such indifference, meaning Punching Crab wondered if Felonious ever really cared about the spirit animals.

"And you were prepared to kill the Akaway?" he asked, secretly hoping that Felonious would have a logical explanation that would make everything seem okay. Unfortunately, hope doesn't always work that way.

"The Akaway has been dead for years," said Felonious, lecturing the entire group as if he were an expert on the topic, which, of course, he was. "Maybe not for real but in spirit. You know that as well as I do. And nothing is going to change that. So why can't a fish get a little piece of the action? Well, now, thanks to these kids, I have my chance. And once we infiltrate the spirit-animal world, who knows how powerful I'll become."

"You know that it takes a very special kid to gain access to the spirit world?" said Punching Crab. "You don't have that."

"Oh, yes we do," said Uncle Skeeta. He turned to Rudy. "Our young partner here is very strong. And he's getting stronger all the time."

Brody looked over at Rudy, who looked right back. And just like that, they both knew they wouldn't be best friends anymore. Now they would be something very different. Uncle Skeeta just smirked and spread his arms as if to ask, "Anything else?"

But there was nothing else to say. It's never good when you realize all your hard work, passion, and perseverance might have actually ended up helping the team you were working so hard to defeat. But if you ever have to experience that feeling, then you might as well experience it while a warm, soft rain is coming down. Because while there's nothing you can do about what just happened, something about the rain might provide the inspiration you need to fight just as hard the next time.

"Well, I'm not going to let that happen," said Jake. Brody's eyes widened with just a hint of optimism as Jake stepped forward and looked Uncle Skeeta right in the eye, in the kind of way that earns respect, especially from your foes.

"You're not?" asked Uncle Skeeta slyly. "Are you trying to tell me that you believe in all of this stuff?"

There was a long pause while Uncle Skeeta and everyone else waited for an answer.

"It doesn't matter what I believe," said Jake.

"Oh, it's so easy to keep saying that, isn't it?" snapped Uncle Skeeta. "But the truth is it matters very much. So we're all listening. Why don't you tell us all, what do you believe?"

Jake thought for a second. He looked to all his friends, then Punching Crab, and finally to Brody, and that's when he knew exactly what to say.

"I don't know. That's what I believe," said Jake. "I may never know. But in the meantime, I'm going to enjoy what

I do know is real, like the fact that we accomplished our mission today, no matter what you say." He paused for a second and thought about adding something nice about his little brother. But he didn't.

Instead, he added, "And I'll tell you one more thing. I like having a spirit animal, whether it's real or not. So I'm going to make sure it stays strong. And I only tell you this because there's really nothing you or Felonious can do about it."

There was a silence among the kids as they tried to digest all Jake had just said. But speeches and spirit animals and brothers sticking together meant very little to Felonious, who just huffed, shook his head, and checked his watch.

"Is that all you got?" asked Felonious, glancing up to the ray of light that was coming from the Illumination.

"Not even close," came a voice from behind the bushes. And out walked a kid wearing an *I'm in charge* T-shirt.

"I'm with them," said Brian.

"Me too," said Jared.

"Me three," said Lainey.

"Me four," said Geovanny.

"Me five," said Cole.

Brian walked over to Brody and stuck out his hand.

"I hope you don't mind that we came," he said. "It was such a great day outside, we thought it might be fun to go on an adventure. You seen any quicksand?"

"But how did you find us?" asked Brody.

"She helped us," said Brian, and he pointed to the path.

That's when Grammy walked out, with a skip in her step, a smile on her face, and a special, super-duper, double-ripple, hot fudge, chocolate pudding birthday cake in her hands. It appeared as though she was floating, but grammies can't float, so we'll just say she was walking confidently, filled with renewed strength, thanks to the energy coming from Sarraka. Following close behind was a four-legged mutt heading right for Jake.

"Tackle!" he yelled, and the dog obeyed, bringing Jake to the ground and slobbering him with doggy kisses.

"Well, I must say, this is beautiful to see," Uncle Skeeta said, checking his watch for the last time. He looked at Grammy and flashed a smile, as if to say, "Nice move with the spit." Or maybe he was saying, "I'm glad you're feeling better." But most likely he was saying, "Good-bye for now." Because at that moment, Uncle Skeeta turned to Rudy, who nodded. He turned to Felonious, who also nodded. Quick as three ninjas, they darted straight ahead into the Illumination, and just like that, they were gone.

With only an instant of hesitation, Jake and Brody sprinted after them, but they hadn't been checking their watches the way Uncle Skeeta had. The portal was open only for six minutes, and Uncle Skeeta had counted those six minutes right down to the last second. So even though Jake and Brody arrived only a few seconds later in the exact same spot as Uncle Skeeta, Felonious, and Rudy, it was a few seconds too late.

"They're gone," said Brody. "What have we done?"

Now You Know

It wasn't until much later that night that Brody Boondoggle, Jake, and Grammy hiked back to the Sequestered Spring so that the Akaway could return home. Brody had invited Jake to come along on the final adventure of his birthday, and Jake had accepted. Maybe it was the start of a new tradition.

They talked very little, except to say things like, "Check out that shooting star" or "Is that a hunter's moon?" or "What could they have been thinking when they named a planet Uranus?"

Jake still couldn't see the Akaway, but hiking at night using only the stars and moon for light, for the first time in his life, he could see the magic. It was all around him.

The Akaway didn't need the light from the Illumination to return home. Now that she was back to full strength, she could come and go as she pleased. But that strength came at a price, and now the Akaway would need all her powers to prepare Sarraka for the uninvited guests that were already a half a day ahead.

Coincidentally or not, Grammy was feeling better as well. She would probably never get her hearing back to full strength, but the rest of her senses were recovering nicely, and she was jumping over logs, cruising through streams, and ducking under branches just like someone whose spirit animal was finally back at full strength.

As for Brody, even a magical hike doesn't help when your instincts are telling you that there's a very good chance everything's not going to turn out okay.

"I'm sorry," Brody whispered to the Akaway when they finally reached the spot of the Illumination. "I'm sorry for the trouble I brought you."

There may never be a time when animals can truly speak the same language as humans. But that doesn't mean they can't communicate with us, and thanks to Brody's special powers, he knew exactly what the Akaway was saying when it lifted its head, leaned in, and did something that only a very few Akaways, in the history of Akaways—and it's a long history—have ever done to a person or animal of any kind.

It licked him.

The Akaway licked Brody right where it had bitten him. And in that instant, the bleeding finally stopped, and Brody heard the voice one more time.

You did not bring trouble, it said. *You brought honor. You brought courage. You made it possible to continue our fight. And that is what we will do.*

And then the Akaway was gone.

There was a long silence, and finally Grammy moved closer to Brody and motioned Jake to move closer as well. She lowered herself down tenderly until she rested on one knee, where she explained how two brothers, sticking together, was one of the most perfect things in the universe.

"Remember, there is magic all around us," she said softly.

Jake smiled. Brody didn't.

"But what about Sarraka?" he said.

"What about it?" asked Grammy.

"It's in danger," said Brody.

"It very well might be," said Grammy. "But I do know that the Akaway would not have survived if you didn't open that portal. Now, it's healthy and strong. And I couldn't imagine a world without an Akaway. Could you?"

Ready to find
YOUR
Spirit Animal?

Visit www.brodyboondoggle.com

Coming Soon:
Two more books
in the Brody Boondoggle Series

The Rock of Sarraka

and

Doctor Dave's Vision

About the Author

Gary Karton came up with the idea for the Brody Boondoggle series after a birthday party he created for his younger son. The party started with a short story about special powers and animals and magic. Then, the kids at the party had to accomplish five fun challenges. If they were successful, they were connected to their spirit animals. The kids loved it (which is more than could be said for some of Gary's other party ideas), and Gary started writing the next day.

Gary began his career as a reporter for *The Washington Post.* He stood out because of an innate ability to unjam the copy machine under deadline pressure. He has spent the past 17 years working for children and families at nonprofits such as the Welfare to Work Partnership, the Elizabeth Glaser Pediatric AIDS Foundation, and Safe Kids Worldwide. He is also the author of *No Free Lunch: One Man's Journey from Welfare to the American Dream* (Ballantine, May 2002).

Gary lives in Virginia with his wife, two sons, and dog.